RANDOM
HOUSE

LARGE
PRINT

Christmas 2017

Dear Friends,

After all these years, you, my readers, have come to expect a Christmas story from me, and I look forward to supplying one. It's one of the many joys I have as a writer. I've always been a Christmas kind of girl. I seem to go overboard every December with multiple lights, decorations, and nativity scenes all around the house. I can't help myself. (Wayne is a tolerant husband.)

This book is dedicated to the couple who purchased our Florida home, with the hopes that they will enjoy it as much as Wayne and I did. It was hard to let it go, but we feel we left this special home in good hands. This last winter Wayne and I decided that instead of wintering in one location, it was time for us to spend part of our winters traveling around the world. We call it our **adventure before dementia.** We already have our trip planned for this winter. We're off to explore the Great Wall of China.

Merry and Bright is a fun story. I hope you have the chance to sit back, prop up your feet, and take a break from the holiday craziness to read it. My wish is that you will smile and it will bring a bit of light and warmth to your winter.

From the time I published my first book, I looked forward to getting mail from my readers. That hasn't changed. You can reach me through my website at debbiemacomber.com or on Facebook, Twitter, or Instagram. Or you can write me at P.O. Box 1458, Port Orchard, WA 98366.

I'll close this by sending you the warmest of holiday greetings.

Merry Christmas.

Debbie Macomber

Angels at the Table
Any Dream Will Do
Blossom Street Brides
Dashing Through the Snow
A Girl's Guide to Moving On
If Not for You
Last One Home
Love Letters
Mr. Miracle
Rose Harbor in Bloom
Silver Linings
Starting Now
Sweet Tomorrows
Twelve Days of Christmas

Merry and Bright

DEBBIE MACOMBER

Merry and Bright

✳

A Novel

RANDOM HOUSE
LARGE PRINT

Copyright © 2017 by Debbie Macomber
Excerpt from **Twelve Days of Christmas** by Debbie Macomber copyright © 2016 by Debbie Macomber

All rights reserved.
Published in the United States of America by Random House Large Print in association with Ballantine Books, an imprint of Random House, a division of Penguin Random House LLC, New York.

Cover design by Lynn Andreozzi
Cover illustrations by Tom Hallman
(based on photographs by C & S Gamble)

The Library of Congress has established a Cataloging-in-Publication record for this title.

ISBN: 978-0-5254-9306-8

www.randomhouse.com/largeprint

FIRST LARGE PRINT EDITION

Printed in the United States of America

10 9 8 7 6 5 4 3 2 1

This Large Print edition published in accord with the standards of the N.A.V.H.

Merry and Bright

CHAPTER ONE

*

Merry

"Mom, I need to work overtime, so I won't be home to help with dinner."

"Again?" her mother moaned into the phone.

"Yes, sorry." Merry hated leaving her mother with the task of cooking dinner. Robin Knight struggled with mobility issues due to complications with multiple sclerosis. As much as Merry hated the thought of it, her mother would soon be confined to a wheelchair.

"That's three nights this week."

Merry didn't need the reminder. Three

nights out of four. Matterson Consulting, the firm where she worked as a temp, was involved in a huge project, its biggest one to date, for the Boeing Company. With the time crunch, everyone on staff was putting in mandatory overtime. Normally, few would object to the extra hours, but the holiday season was right around the corner. People were busy planning parties, shopping for gifts, decorating, baking, and making holiday plans to visit families. All the normal, fun things that were part of this time of year, but for those employed by Matterson, it didn't matter. Christmas might as well be blocked off the calendar.

"Don't worry, dear," Merry's mother assured her gently. "Patrick will help me with dinner."

Merry closed her eyes and let her shoulders sag. Patrick was a dear boy, but he tended to dirty every dish in the house when he cooked. Her eighteen-year-old Down syndrome brother was the light of her life, but his help in the kitchen was questionable at best.

"Heat up soup and have Patrick make sandwiches," Merry suggested.

"We can do that, but you should know Bogie is out of dog food."

Bogie was Patrick's golden retriever, who had an appetite that rivaled that of an entire high school football squad. Grocery shopping was a task Merry had taken on as her mother's illness progressed. However, working the hours she did made it nearly impossible to find the time needed. "Oh Mom, I'm sorry. Poor Bogie. I'll stop off at the store on my way home and pick some up." While she was there she'd grab a few other essentials, too, like milk and bread. They were running low on both. And maybe some ice cream for Patrick, who never complained about the need to help his mother.

"Your father can do that on his way home—"

"Don't ask Dad," Merry interrupted. Her father was in pharmaceutical sales and traveled extensively around the Pacific Northwest and was often on the road. He carried a heavy enough load as it was. By the time he got home from driving across the state, he'd be exhausted. Merry didn't want to burden him with any extra chores. Buying the groceries was her responsibility.

Everyone worked together in the Knight family. They were a tight-knit group by necessity and by love. Merry had taken the twelve-month temp job with Matterson Consulting to save tuition money for college. Her educational expenses were more than their family budget could manage. She'd been hired by Matterson Consulting specifically for this Boeing project and had worked extensively on inputting the data. It'd taken months to accumulate all the necessary information. It was all

winding down now. December 23 would
be her last day on the job.

After working with the company for
nearly a year, she'd made friends with
the other two women working in data
entry. They considered her part of the
team and often turned to her with questions, as she had replaced the department
head. Although she was only a temporary
employee, her skill level was above those
currently assigned to the project.

Merry took another bite of the peanut-
butter sandwich she'd brought for lunch.
She usually ate at her desk and worked
through her lunch break. Most everyone
else went to a local café around the corner,
where the food was fast, cheap, and tasty.
All three were necessary if Merry was
going to splurge and eat out. She treated
herself once a week, but more often than
that would play havoc with her budget.
Most days she brown-bagged it.

"When was the last time you went out, Merry?" her mother asked.

"I go out every day," she answered, sidestepping the question.

"On a date."

"Mom! When do I have time to date?" Merry had a fairly good idea what had prompted the question. Her best friend from high school had recently announced she was pregnant.

"That's exactly my point. You're twenty-four years old and you're living the life of a nun."

"Mom!"

"Patrick dates more than you do."

Merry had to smile, even though her mother was right. Her younger brother was involved with a special group that held dances and other events that allowed him to socialize with other teens who had Down syndrome. As a high school senior, he was active in drama and part of the football team. He had a girlfriend as well.

"It's time you stopped worrying about your family and had some fun."

"I have fun," Merry countered. She had friends, and while she didn't see them often, they were in touch via social media, email, and texting. If Merry was busy, which she tended to be, then she communicated with emojis. It was fun to see how much she could say with a simple symbol or two.

"Have you ever thought about joining one of those online matchmaking sites?" her mother asked, sounding thoughtful.

"No," Merry returned emphatically, rolling her eyes. She hoped the state of her social life would change once she could afford to return to school. It wasn't like she was a martyr, but at times she struggled with the weight of family obligations. She tried not to think about everything she was missing that her friends enjoyed. It was what it was, and it didn't do any good to feel sorry for herself. Her family needed her.

"Why don't you try it? It'd be fun."

"Mom, have you seen all the forms and questionnaires that need to be filled out for those dating sites? I don't have time for that." **Especially now, with the demands of my job,** she thought to herself.

"Make time."

"I will someday," she said, hoping that would appease her mother.

"**Someday,** Merry? Failing to plan is planning to fail."

"Mom. You sound like Anthony Robbins." Although she complained, her mother was right. The timing, however, was all wrong.

"I'll think about it after the first of the year," she promised.

Her best friend Dakota had met the love of her life online at Mix & Mingle.

Inspired by Dakota's success, Merry had checked out the site, but she became bogged down with the page upon page of questions that needed to be completed. She started filling out the forms but quickly gave up, exasperated by all the busywork.

"You need to get out more, enjoy life," her mother continued. "There's more to life than work and more work."

"I agree. After the holidays. Let me finish this temp job first."

"It worked for Dakota."

"Mom, please. I have plenty of time to get out there." Merry didn't need the reminder about her friend's happy ending. After Dakota met Michael on the site, she had sung the website's praises to Merry like a wolf howling at the moon. She wouldn't stop bugging Merry about it until she'd promised to give it a try.

"I heard from her mother this morning. Did you know Dakota and Michael are expecting?"

"Yes, Mom, I heard." Merry reached for her sandwich and was about to take another bite when the vice president of the company, Jayson Bright, walked past her desk. He had to be one of the most serious-minded men Merry had ever met. To the best of her memory she had never seen the man smile. Not once. He looked about as happy as someone scheduled for a root canal.

Jayson Bright paused and stared at Merry. His eyes fell to the nameplate on her desk. MARY KNIGHT. She'd asked HR to correct the spelling of her first name twice, with no success, and then gave up. Seeing that she was a temp, they hadn't shown that much interest. Her boss's gaze landed on the sandwich she had on her desk, and for a moment she toyed with the idea of offering him half, but as she doubted he'd find any humor in it, she restrained herself. He arched his brows before he walked away.

"Merry, did you hear me?" her mother asked.

"Sorry, no, I was distracted." From Mr. Bright's look, Merry had to wonder if there was something written in the employee handbook about eating at her desk. She'd been doing it for almost a full year now, and no one had mentioned that it was frowned upon before.

"Merry?"

"Mom. I need to get off the phone. I'll call you before I leave the office."

"Okay, but think about what I said, all right?"

"I will, Mom." Merry's mind filled with visions of meeting her own Prince Charming. Of one thing she was certain: It wouldn't be someone as dour as Jayson Bright.

Sure enough, just as Merry suspected, at three that same afternoon, a notice was sent around the office.

It is preferred that all staff refrain from eating at their desks. For those who choose to remain in the office for lunch, a designated room is provided. Thank you.

Jayson Bright
Vice President
Matterson Consulting

Merry read the email and instinctively knew that this edict was directed at her. She preferred to avoid the lunchroom, and with good reason. The space was often crowded and it was uncomfortable bumbling around, scooting between those at the tables and those waiting in line for a turn at the microwave. Besides, it was more efficient to eat at her desk. Not that Mr. Bright seemed to notice or care.

What a shame—the company vice president was such a curmudgeon. Merry had heard women in the office claim he was hot. She agreed. Jayson Bright was hot, all right. Hotheaded! He was young for his position as vice president. The rumor mill in the office said he was related to the Matterson family; the company president was his uncle. Bright would assume the role when it came time for his uncle to retire. His uncle would continue as chairman of the board.

Merry's thoughts drifted to Jayson Bright and she mused at how attractive he would be if he smiled. He was about six feet tall, several inches taller than her five-five, with dark brown hair and eyes. He kept his hair cut in a crisp professional style. Wanting to be generous in spirit, Merry supposed he carried a heavy responsibility. Word was that Jayson Bright was the one responsible for obtaining this Boeing contract. A lot weighed in the balance for him with his job. Merry knew that he put in as many hours, or more, than the rest of the staff.

By the time Merry arrived at home, hauling a ten-pound bag of Bogie's favorite dog food, it was after eight o'clock. As soon as she walked in the door, Patrick rushed to help her with the heavy sack.

His sweet, boyish face was bright with enthusiasm. "Merry's home," he shouted, taking the dog food out of her hands and carting it to the kitchen pantry.

"Hi, sweetheart," her mother called. Her mom leaned heavily on her walker, now exhausted and fatigued, because she grew tired at the end of each day.

"Can I tell her?" Patrick asked excitedly.

"In a minute," her mother said. Merry noticed that her lips quirked in an effort to hold in a smile.

"Tell me what?"

"We got you an early birthday gift this afternoon and it's the best one ever." Patrick rubbed his hands together, unable to disguise his eagerness.

"You did?" Knowing the family budget was tight, Merry wasn't expecting much. Born on December 26, the day after Christmas, Merry had felt cheated as a child when it came to her birthday gifts. Her parents had done their best to make her birthday special, but it being so soon after Christmas made that difficult. It wasn't unusual for Merry to get her birthday gifts early because of it.

"And you're going to be so happy," Patrick assured her. "I helped Mom with everything."

"You helped pick it out?" Merry asked. The two of them must have ordered something off the Internet, because her mother was no longer able to drive and Patrick couldn't. Those with Down syndrome could legally drive in Washington State, but the family couldn't afford a second car. The family had only the one car, which her father used for work. Merry used public transportation to and from her job.

"Well, this isn't something we picked out. You need to do the picking."

"Patrick," his mother chastised. "You're going to give it away."

"You can show me after you feed Bogie," Merry suggested, as Bogie eyed the pantry door.

"We can't really give it to you yet," Patrick told her. "You get to pick for yourself, but I'll help if you want." From the way his eyes lit up, Merry knew he'd be terribly disappointed if he didn't get a say in this.

Okay, now Merry was willing to admit she was intrigued. It was still November, over Thanksgiving weekend. Her brother was barely able to contain himself and rushed to grab Bogie's food dish. She enjoyed his enthusiasm. Seeing the happy anticipation in him piqued her own. She couldn't imagine what this special birth-day gift could possibly be.

Bogie pranced around in his eagerness for Patrick to fill the dish so he could eat.

"Now, Mom, now?" Patrick asked, jumping up and down after he poured the dog food into the bowl. Between the dog and her brother, the two looked like they were doing a square dance.

"Let me eat dinner first," Merry said, teasing her brother.

Patrick's eyes rounded. "Merry, no, please. I've been waiting and waiting to tell you. I don't think I can wait any longer." Merry and her mother shared a smile.

"Have pity on the boy," her mother urged.

Holding back a smile would have been impossible. "Okay, Patrick, you can tell me about my birthday gift."

Her brother's eyes lit up like Fourth of July sparklers. Whatever this early birth-day present was must be special. Merry hugged her brother and, wrapping her arms around his torso, she gave him a gentle squeeze.

Patrick took hold of her hand while their mother opened the laptop and pulled out a chair to sit down. Merry joined her mother.

"You ready?" Robin Knight asked, turning on the computer.

"I can hardly wait," Merry answered.

Tucking his arm around her elbow, Patrick scooted close to Merry.

She looked at the blank computer screen, getting more curious by the second. They both seemed to be squirming with anticipation. "What did you two order me?"

Patrick laughed and pointed to the computer, crying out, "We got you a **man** for your birthday!"

"What?" Merry asked, certain there was some misunderstanding. "I don't think it's possible to buy me a man."

"Not exactly buy," her mother explained. "Patrick and I spent the afternoon online answering the questionnaire for Mix & Mingle. We filled in your profile and signed you up for the next six months."

Merry was speechless for several moments. **"You did what?"**

"We got you a date," Patrick answered, beaming her a huge smile.

If she wasn't already sitting, Merry would have needed to take a seat. Her immediate thought was how best not to disappoint her mother and brother by telling them this wasn't anything she wanted. That thought was quickly followed by a question. "What photo did you use?" She hoped it was a recent one and not some high school prom picture. She'd changed a lot since her teen years. She wore contacts now instead of glasses, which showed off her deep brown eyes; her hair was longer now, shoulder length, parted in the middle. She'd be mortified if they'd used the photo on her employee badge for Matterson Consulting, where she looked like a deer caught in the headlights. Actually, it resembled more of a mug shot.

"That's the best part," Patrick told her, looking well pleased with himself. "We didn't use a photo of you."

Now Merry was totally baffled. "You mean to say you posted a picture of someone else?"

"Don't be silly," her mother responded.

"Well, if it isn't me, then whose photo did you use?"

Patrick's glee couldn't be contained. "We used Bogie's."

"You made me a dog?" Merry cried, resisting the urge to cover her face. "Why?"

"Two reasons," her mother explained.

"One," Patrick intervened, thrusting his index finger into the air, ready to show his reasoning. "You love dogs."

"Ah . . . I guess," Merry admitted. Bogie was as much her dog as Patrick's. He often slept on her bed. She took him for walks on the days Patrick couldn't. Bogie was considered part of the Knight family.

"And second, and most important," her mother continued, "You're a beautiful young woman. Too many potential dates would judge you purely on your looks. That didn't sit right with me. I wanted them to get to know you as a person, as the generous, kindhearted, loving woman you are. They will need to dig deeper into your profile rather than to simply gaze at a photograph. And," she added, "We weren't sure how you'd feel about all of this, so we chose a pseudonym for your name. You are now Merry Smith."

"Merry Smith," she repeated slowly, still having trouble taking all this in. Looking at her profile as it came up on the screen, she withheld a groan. Seeing

Bogie with her pseudonym listed below, she figured it was highly unlikely anyone would send her a Mix & Mingle message. Anyone looking at the photo would think her profile was all one big joke. No one wanted to date a dog.

CHAPTER TWO

Jayson

Jayson Bright walked into his penthouse condo, which had a sweeping view of Puget Sound, and headed directly to his liquor cabinet. It'd been a hellish day. His uncle had been on Jayson's back about this Boeing contract from the moment he stepped into the office that morning. For the thousandth time, Jayson assured his uncle Matt that all was well and that the report would be on time before the Christmas deadline. All he could do was hope that he wasn't blowing smoke. It felt as if his entire future with the company hung in the balance.

Jayson poured himself a glass of his favorite Malbec and sank onto the sofa, resting his head against the back cushion. He took in several deep breaths, doing his best to ease the tension between his shoulder blades. With pressure mounting, he'd been at the office for twelve straight hours and had skipped lunch. By six-thirty he was ravenous. Rather than wait until he was home, he grabbed a sandwich and a latte on his way out of the Fourth Avenue high-rise. This wasn't how he intended to live the rest of his life, and yet it was all he'd known since he'd accepted this position with his uncle's company.

His phone vibrated inside his suit jacket, reminding him that he'd turned off the ringer for the last meeting of the day.

"Yeah," he said, exhausted. It was Cooper, his cousin on his mother's side.

"Hey Jay, is that any way to greet me?"

Despite how tired he was, Jayson grinned. "Where are you, man?" Cooper lived in the San Francisco Bay area. They got together when they could, which wasn't nearly enough to suit either of them. They were the same age and had always been close. Cooper was as close as a brother to Jayson.

"I'm in town."

Jayson sat up straight. "Seattle?"

"Yeah. Technically, the airport. I just stepped off the flight. I'm on my way back from a business trip and got a layover in Seattle."

This was a shock. Had Jayson known, he would have sent a car to get Cooper. "You should have told me you were coming."

"I did. I sent you two texts and left a voice mail. What more do you want?" Cooper razzed.

Jayson set his wineglass aside and wiped

his face. "I was in a meeting and had my phone on vibrate."

"I'll get a cab and be to your place in thirty."

"Perfect." As tired as he'd been, Jayson felt refreshed and eager to see his best friend. It'd been three months since they'd last seen each other, and it felt like a year or longer.

Sure enough, a half-hour later, Jayson let his cousin into the condo. The two pumped fists and then hugged, slapping each other across the back.

After their greeting, Cooper paused and stared out at the sweeping view of the waterfront, lit up with sparkling lights. All too familiar with the view, Jayson barely noticed the scene. The white-and-green ferry gliding across the dark waters of Puget Sound looked like a beacon steering toward Bremerton. The entire Seattle waterfront was lit up in a festive holiday scene.

"I got to tell you, bro, this view gets me every time. It's even more breathtaking with all the Christmas lights."

Christmas.

Jayson didn't want to think about it. It was a month away now, and the pressure was on. Not for the holidays, but for this report the CEO of Boeing was expecting on his desk before the holidays.

Jayson frowned and stared at it himself, then shrugged. "It's okay."

"What?" Cooper cried. "You have one of the most fantastic views in the world and you show no appreciation."

Jayson shrugged. "By the time I get home, I'm too tired to give a damn. Too tired to even notice." It'd been this way ever since his move to Seattle.

His cousin shook his head as though he couldn't believe what he was hearing. "Jay, listen, it's time to stop and smell the roses."

Jayson cracked a smile. "Someday."

Frankly, he didn't see any roses, and even if he did, he wasn't about to stop and take a whiff. His life was busy. He was in the middle of an important assignment and he didn't have time to enjoy the view—or anything else, for that matter.

"Wine?" Jayson asked, diverting Cooper's attention away from the nighttime panorama.

"Sure."

Jayson poured a glass of the rich red Malbec and handed it to his best friend. They clicked glasses and each took a sip.

"Hey, this is good. California?" Cooper asked.

"No, this is from Argentina. The Mendoza area."

Cooper took another sip and said, "I should have known."

Jayson and Cooper were wine snobs and tried to best each other with their out-of-the-way finds. Jayson enjoyed finding small boutique wineries from around the world. It wasn't uncommon for him to order wine for himself and for his cousin and have a case delivered to Cooper's California home. Jayson's biggest coup came when he found a sauvignon blanc at a winery that was practically in Cooper's backyard.

"So what brings you to town?" Jayson asked, taking a seat on his sofa.

His cousin sat on the edge of the cushion on the recliner next to the fireplace. "I'm in love."

Jayson nearly spewed his wine back into the glass. For a long moment, he stared at his cousin to be sure this wasn't a joke. "What? You're in love? I know you said you were dating a new girl, but love? How did this happen?"

"How?" Cooper repeated, grinning like a schoolboy. "You're acting like I caught some sort of infectious disease."

Years ago, they had made a promise to each other not to marry before they were forty. If then. Both sets of their parents had been through multiple marriages. They decided they'd be smarter than their parents. If and when they ever **did** fall in love, it would be when they were mature enough to know what they wanted.

"Are you sure it's love?" Jayson found it hard to believe. He could tell this wasn't a joke. Cooper was as serious as an undertaker.

"She's got me—hook, line, and sinker."

Jayson rolled his eyes. "I can't believe this. Next thing I know you're going to tell me you're getting married."

In response, Cooper arched his brows.

Jayson froze. "You kidding me, man."

"No. Flew here to ask you to be my best man at the wedding."

Too stunned to react, Jayson remained speechless as his mind whirled with the question. "You're serious? You're really going to do it?"

"Yup."

"This girl's family's not blackmailing you? This is completely voluntary?"

"Completely voluntary," Cooper repeated, grinning at the question. "Fact is, I can't wait to make Maddy my wife."

Jayson slouched against the sofa in disbelief. Something was up. This wasn't the Cooper he knew as well as he knew himself. There had to be a catch to all this. Frowning, he said, "I've got to meet this woman. This Maddy must really be something to knock you off your feet."

"You have met her. Remember Maddy Baldwin? She attended boarding school and camp with us."

Jayson bolted to his feet and brushed the hair from his forehead. "Maddy Baldwin? The girl who was a major pain in the butt?"

"Yup, her."

Jayson knew exactly who Maddy was. He'd spent one entire summer with her at an East Coast camp. Both Jayson and

Cooper were more of an inconvenience to their parents, so as soon as they were old enough to be shipped to boarding school, off they went. During the summers, it was camp. They rarely had any contact with their parents. When they did, it was a disappointment. The cousins had each other, and they became their own family.

"Man, you've got to be kidding me. The Maddy I remember had red hair and braces on her buck teeth. She drove us both nuts."

"That she did."

"I thought she moved to California after her sophomore year?"

"She did."

"You kept in touch with her?" Surely Cooper would have mentioned it before now if he had. As a twelve-year-old, she'd been a major pest. She was a tomboy and always wanted to join in on their fun. Despite everything the two had done to ditch her, Maddy would inevitably find them. That entire summer she'd been a constant thorn in their side. The girl simply wouldn't take no for an answer.

"We found each other six months ago and hit it off. It didn't take long for me to realize she's the one. Trust me, the buck teeth are gone. You wouldn't recognize her these days. I'm telling you, Maddy's a knockout." Cooper reached for his phone and brought up a current photo.

His cousin wasn't exaggerating. Maddy was a looker, all right. Jayson blinked a couple times, hardly able to believe this was the same Maddy who'd plagued them all those years ago. "That's Maddy?"

"Yup. I gotta tell you, cuz, the minute we connected, I felt something right here." He pressed his hand over his heart and patted it several times. "I never told you, but back at camp she was my first kiss and I was hers."

"You kissed her? No way." Jayson shook his head, finding this confession more than a little shocking.

"It was after you left camp. Maddy offered to pay me."

Jayson burst out laughing.

"No joke. She wanted to know what it was like to be kissed and offered me five bucks. I'm no fool—I took it. I mean, it wasn't going to hurt any, and frankly, I was a little curious myself. We did the deed and then she demanded a refund because, in her words, it was gross."

"Did you return her money?"

"No way. I fulfilled my part of the bargain. I told her if she felt cheated she could take it up with an attorney."

Jayson rubbed his hand down his face. He found it difficult to believe his closest friend and cousin loved a woman enough to marry her. "How did you two reconnect?"

"You aren't going to believe this."

At this point, Jayson was ready to believe just about anything. "Tell me."

"I saw her on Mix & Mingle."

The last thing his cousin needed was help finding dates. Cooper was a magnet when it came to attractive women. "Mix & Mingle? Isn't that an online dating site? What were **you** doing on a dating site?"

"No, not me. One of the guys from the office was on the site and looking at profiles. He asked me to look with him. You remember Doug, don't you? Nerdy guy, thick glasses. A computer genius, but when it comes to women he was a total loser. He signed up, and once he had all these women's profiles to review, he got overwhelmed. I told him I'd help him find the perfect woman for him. Finding Maddy on that site was my destiny."

"You stumbled upon Maddy's profile?"

"I saw the name before I saw the photo. Couldn't believe it when I realized this was Maddy. Our Maddy. Then I found the woman I thought Doug would like, and as a thank-you, he let me send Maddy a message. She remembered me, too, and answered back. As they say, the rest is history."

Jayson remained suspicious. "If Maddy's so hot, why'd she resort to an online dating site?"

"I asked her the same thing. She'd been batting zero in the romance department. No time, working crazy hours, but then a friend talked her into it. Naturally, she was skeptical, but she decided to give it a try."

"What does she do?"

"Maddy's a doctor."

"A doctor. Maddy?"

"Yes, and she's amazing. I can't wait for you two to talk. The minute you see her, you'll know why I decided she's the one."

Jayson raised his glass for a toast and Cooper touched the rim of the wineglass with his own. "To craziness, marriage, and finding love when least expected."

"Hear, hear."

They both took a healthy swallow of the wine.

"When's the wedding?"

"Not until September. Maddy thought we'd get married in a vineyard, seeing how we both share a love of wine."

"Great idea." He could picture the scene in his mind, with the rolling hills of vines in the background. Any number of beautiful spots in California wine country would be a great setting for a wedding.

"In New Zealand."

Jayson laughed. "A destination wedding."

"You'll make it, won't you? Clear your schedule now."

No question Jayson would be there. If need be, he'd willingly fly to the moon for this wedding. "I wouldn't miss it for the world."

"Great. Then you'll agree to serve as my best man?"

"I'll consider it an honor."

Cooper spent the night and then took an early-morning flight back to San Francisco the following day. It was a good thing Jayson's cousin had delivered the news in person. If Cooper had told him over the phone, Jayson would never have believed him. He would have been convinced it was a hoax.

As Jayson dressed in his usual suit and tie for work the next morning, he realized he'd been so caught up in work that he hadn't gone out socially in several weeks. His relationships were nonexistent, especially since he started working for his uncle. He rarely dated the same woman more than a few times.

Like his cousin, he'd never had trouble connecting with women. Six feet, broad shoulders, dark hair and eyes. No one needed to tell him he stood out in a crowd. The problem was that most women were attracted to his name and his wealth. He was continually left in doubt if their feelings for him were genuine. He was considered a prize catch. He wasn't being vain; it was just the plain truth. Humility had nothing to do with it.

Out of curiosity and more than any need or desire to date, Jayson decided to log on to the website for Mix & Mingle and searched for the photos of women who'd signed up in the Seattle area.

Immediately he saw row upon row of photos. He was ready to exit the site when something different caught his eye. Instead of a woman, there was a picture of a dog.

A golden retriever.

He looked again to be sure he wasn't seeing things. Yup, it was a dog.

He couldn't imagine why someone

would put up a photo of a dog. For several moments, he mulled it over and was unable to come up with an answer. He figured he'd wasted enough time, shut down his laptop, and headed for the office.

Friday finally arrived and Jayson should have been thinking about something other than work. His friends, few of them as there were, would be going out, enjoying themselves. But anything social wasn't in the cards for him.

Later in the afternoon as the workday was winding down, his scheduled conference call was canceled. He had a few minutes, and for no reason he could name, he went back to the Mix & Mingle website.

The photo of the dog was still up. Again, he stared at it, and as he did, the thought came to him that maybe the woman who'd posted it was like him. A woman who put more stock in character than in looks or position.

Her profile listed her name.

Merry Smith.

Clearly that was made up, and he suspected her first name referenced Christmas, which was interesting.

The dog in the photo was cute. Jayson had a dog once. Rocky had been a golden retriever like this one. His dad had bought Rocky for him when Jayson briefly lived with him. During his junior year, his mother had a fit of guilt and insisted he finish high school living with her rather than his father. Unfortunately, Jayson didn't get along with his new stepdad, so his mother had shipped him back to live with his father. It wouldn't have been so bad, except his stepmother wasn't that keen on him, either. Jayson spent a miserable two years with his father. The only thing that helped him through that time was Rockefeller, or Rocky, his dog. He stared at the photo for several minutes and then closed the site.

By the time he left the office, Jayson discovered only a few staff voluntarily stayed behind to work the overtime hours that had been approved to finish this Boeing contract on time. It wasn't mandatory on Friday night, and Jayson appreciated those who were willing to work when it wasn't required.

As he headed toward his condo, Jayson couldn't help but think back to the website and to the woman behind the dog. He wanted to know more. His curiosity got the best of him and he spent an hour filling out the questionnaire. Even as he filled in the answers, he suspected it would be a complete waste of time. When it came to inserting his photograph, he found an old photo of Rocky and posted it.

Pleased with himself, he shut down his laptop. Maybe later, if he felt like it, he'd send Merry Smith a message and see how it played out.

CHAPTER THREE

✳

Merry

It was after seven by the time Merry arrived home from work the following Monday. As soon as she walked into the kitchen, Patrick looked up from the laptop on the table and shot her a wide, happy grin.

"Merry, you got a wink on Mix & Mingle! His name is Jay and he likes you."

Not wanting to disappoint her brother, Merry swallowed a groan. As a matter of fact, she'd received several "winks" on the dating website, most of which told humorous tales of having dated other dogs.

But in the end, the winks told Merry they weren't interested in actually meeting her. Why these men even bothered to contact her remained a mystery—one she would rather not explore. In a way, her mother had been right. Putting up the photo of Bogie helped filter out those who would be a poor match. Those heartless winks told her as much.

Robin Knight sat in the family room. "This guy looks promising," she called out in a happy, singsong voice.

Patrick nodded enthusiastically. "If you look at his photo, you'll like him, too," her brother insisted, his eyes twinkling with delight. Bogie, his faithful companion, was at his side and stared up at the computer screen alongside Patrick. Bogie cocked his head to one side as if intrigued himself.

"Give me a minute to unwind," Merry pleaded.

"You need to answer him," Patrick insisted.

"Later . . . okay?"

"Do it now," her brother tried again, his eyes wide and hopeful. "Just look at his picture."

Merry glanced over and blinked. Twice. "He sent the picture of a dog?"

"It's a handsome dog. A golden retriever like Bogie."

Her mother gave her the look. It was one Merry had learned to recognize— the look that said if Merry didn't follow through, then she would be disappointing Patrick.

"I like Jay," Patrick said.

"Okay, okay," Merry muttered, giving in. No wonder her family was intrigued, and she had to admit that now she was, too.

After heating up leftover meatloaf and scalloped potatoes, Merry sat down next to Patrick, prepared to send her first message.

"What should I say?" she asked her brother, seeking inspiration.

Patrick mulled over the question. "Tell him you like his photo."

Merry grinned and set her fingers on the keyboard and typed.

Bow wow.

Along with her message, the picture of Bogie showed up on the screen so he'd know it was her.

Patrick read Merry's message and laughed.

Almost right away a response came through, as if he'd been sitting in front of his computer, waiting for her.

Bow wow back.

You have a dog, too?

Not anymore. The photo is of Rocky. Had him as a teenager. He died while I was away at college. Still miss him.

You didn't get another dog?

No. Hate to leave one cooped up in a condo all day. Not fair to him.

I agree. Bogie is a family dog.

You done this dating-website thing before?

Never. A first for me. You?

Me, neither. Feeling a little foolish, actually.

Understand. Me, too.

Patrick continued to sit at Merry's side and read their exchange. "Tell him that Mom and I signed you up for your birthday gift."

"Okay."

My teenage brother signed me up for this as a birthday gift.

Something you wanted?

Yes and no. Busy with work. Don't have time for a social life.

Same here.

What prompted you to sign up on Mix & Mingle?

Best friend met the love of his life on

here. Curiosity got the better of me. Figured it'd be a waste of time.

Then what made you go through with it?

You.

Me?

The answer made Merry sit up and take notice.

Delighted, Patrick clapped his hands. "Mom and I did good, didn't we?"

"Looks that way," Merry agreed.

You and the photo of your dog. Reminded me of Rocky.

Merry paused to take a bite of her dinner. Before she could respond, Jay sent another note.

Your profile intrigued me.

Remember, my brother is the one who filled it out. I have to admit, I didn't read it over.

You don't know if it's true or not?

Oh, I'm sure it is true. Patrick is honest to a fault.

"Tell him I'm special," her brother said,

leaning forward and balancing his elbows on the tabletop.

"Okay, okay."

Patrick wants me to tell you he's "special," if you know what I mean. He's a great kid and works at a local grocery store.

A pause followed, as if Jay was trying to read between the lines.

How old is Patrick?

He's eighteen/twelve.

Gotcha.

Worked ten hours today. It's time for a hot bath and bed.

Hear you. Would you like to chat again?

Merry read the line twice.

"Tell him yes," Patrick urged. "He didn't make any bad jokes about you being a dog or anything."

Bogie seemed to agree. He rested his chin on Merry's thigh as though to urge her.

Sure. When?

Tomorrow night. Same time?

Okay.

Merry closed the computer and leaned back in the chair.

"Well, what do you think?" her mother asked.

Merry was surprised to realize she was interested in getting to know Jay better. When she'd learned what her mother and Patrick had done, she'd been convinced it had been a waste of time and their limited funds. She never expected anything to come of it. And it very well might not. She'd chatted with one guy. Just one. The other "winks" were from men she wouldn't seriously consider meeting.

Merry got out of the office later than normal on Tuesday night. She'd told her new Mix & Mingle friend, Jay, that they could connect around the same time, and she was thirty minutes behind schedule. Being on time had been drilled into her from when she was young, and she hated the thought of being late. For Jay. For anyone.

Rushing in the front door, she shucked off her coat and headed to the kitchen to find both her mother and Patrick leaning over the laptop set up on the round table.

"I need to log on for Jay," she said, anxious now.

"Patrick and I are talking to him," her mother said, looking pleased with herself.

"What?" Her fear was that they were pretending to be her, which would be disastrous. She could only imagine what they would say, and she inwardly groaned.

"No, no—Patrick and I let Jay know it was us. We didn't want to keep him waiting," her mother explained, as if she was only doing what was necessary. "Otherwise he might think you aren't interested, and you are."

Merry was anxious to chat with Jay again. "What did you tell him?"

"Nothing much. Just that you had texted to say that you were late getting out of the office."

Her heart was pounding as Patrick slid out of his chair for her to get in front of the computer. "You can take over now."

"Thanks."

"I like him, Merry," her mother said. "He seems polite and nice."

Having her mother and Patrick's seal of approval went a long way toward making her more comfortable with Jay.

I just stepped in the door. So sorry to be late.

Enjoyed the chat with your mom and Patrick. They sang your praises.

Don't believe everything they said. On second thought, please do. I'm tall, thin, and gorgeous. That's what they said, right?

Close. Were you out Christmas shopping?

No, work again. Mandatory overtime.

Same. I'm still at the office.

Oh no. Hope you don't have a long commute.

Not at all.

Good.

Good day for you?

Fairly good. Not a fan of my boss and grateful I didn't see him today. I think he might be out of the office. How about you?

Meetings all day. Found my thoughts drifting a few times, thinking about our chat. Gave me something to look forward to this evening.

I felt the same way.

Merry sat at her computer for an hour as they typed messages back and forth. He asked and answered question after question. From his responses, she could see that he was becoming more relaxed with her. She was beginning to be more at ease with him, too.

Wednesday night Merry spent another hour online with Jay. This time she took the laptop into her bedroom and sat on her bed with her back against her headboard and the computer balanced on her lap as she typed away. About thirty minutes into their exchange, Patrick knocked on her bedroom door.

"Yeah?"

Her brother stuck his head into her room. "Tell Jay I said hello. Okay?"

"Okay." Her fingers flew across the keys.

Patrick wants me to tell you hello. Of all the men who winked at me, he likes you the best.

You got a lot of winks?

A few. She didn't mention they were mostly making fun of her dog picture with no real interest in her. You?

A few.

More than three?

Way more.

Really. How many is way more? Four?

Ha, ha.

Okay, I give up. How many?

A dozen.

That's a joke, right?

Hey, a handsome guy like myself is a real find.

Merry couldn't keep the smile off her face.

After an hour had passed, they set an earlier time for Friday to chat again.

All day Friday Merry found herself glancing at the clock every few minutes as it neared five o'clock. She didn't want to be late the way she had been on Tuesday. Thankfully, her boss had made Fridays an exception to the mandatory overtime. The minute it was five o'clock, Merry started clearing off her desk, eager to escape.

Kylie, one of the other data entry workers, was in an even bigger rush to get out of the office.

"How's Palmer today?" Merry asked.

Kylie's three-year-old, Palmer, had come down with the flu and she'd been up half the night with him. She'd phoned in sick, but when Jayson Bright got wind that the department was one person short, he'd come unglued. Not that he'd shouted or made a scene. That wasn't his way. He'd personally contacted Kylie and explained that it was vital that this report be finished before Christmas. She was needed at the office and he wasn't willing to accept excuses. Her son would be perfectly fine with a babysitter.

Kylie had tried to argue, but the heartless Mr. Bright had given her the choice: a babysitter for her son or her job. Fortunately, at the last minute Kylie's mother had been able to look after the little boy.

Merry had been angry on Kylie's behalf. As far as she was concerned, the man was heartless and unreasonable and had his priorities askew. Even worse, he wouldn't allow personal phone calls on company time. While that was standard for most workplaces, extenuating circumstances did occur, like a sick three-year-old.

Kylie had her phone pressed to her ear, checking up on her son, as she raced toward the elevator ahead of Merry and Lauren, who sat at the desk closest to Merry.

For that matter, Merry was in a hurry to get away herself.

"Hey, what's the big rush?" Lauren asked. "You got a hot Friday-night date?"

"Sort of." Merry grabbed her purse from beneath her desk and slung the strap over her shoulder.

"How do you **sort of** have a hot date?"

"I'm talking to a guy I met online."

Lauren whistled softly. "Oh yeah. Where's all that complaining and grumbling you did after your mom and Patrick signed you up for that dating site? I see you're singing a different tune now."

"This guy sounds great."

Lauren had yet to be convinced this was a good way to meet somebody. At forty-five, she'd been divorced ten years and had given up on men and romance. "**Sounds** great?"

"Yeah, his profile picture was a golden retriever, too."

"You mean to say you don't know what he looks like?"

"No," Merry said, unruffled by her friend's concern. "Remember, he doesn't know what I look like, either, so we're both taking a chance."

Lauren remained skeptical. "He could be fat and fifty."

"He isn't." Merry wasn't sure why she was so confident of this. Jay sounded young, and he hit all the right notes with her. She chose to believe he was everything he said he was.

Lauren squinted her eyes. "How do you know?"

Unable to explain her gut feeling, Merry shrugged. "I can tell."

"Has he suggested you meet yet?" Lauren asked as they walked to the elevator.

"No." But she hadn't, either. They were in the getting-to-know-you stage. No need to rush this, especially when they both seemed to be heavily involved with work.

Lauren arched her finely trimmed eyebrows as if that said it all.

"You're far too skeptical," Merry complained as she pressed the down button. "We've only messaged a few times. It's too early. I want to know more about him before I'm willing to do a face-to-face." Although he hadn't said it, Merry was sure Jay felt the same way. It was far too soon in their relationship.

The elevator door slipped open and Merry and Lauren stepped inside. Lauren pushed the button for the lobby.

"Hold that door," Jayson Bright shouted as he raced across the floor, weaving his way around desks while shoving his arm into the sleeve of his three-quarter-length raincoat.

This was the man who had been unrelenting when it came to these long mandatory hours of overtime. He'd been unwilling to listen to excuses for time off. Even for a sick child.

Heartless.

Demanding.

Unreasonable.

If it was up to Merry she would have let the elevator door close in his face.

Lauren apparently didn't share her dislike of their boss. She thrust out her arm, which caused the automatic door to glide back open.

"Thanks." Jayson Bright joined them.

Standing behind him, Merry made a face. She put her thumbs in her ears and wiggled them back and forth while sticking out her tongue at him.

Stifling a giggle, Lauren cupped her hand over her mouth.

One floor down, the elevator stopped again. Jayson stepped aside to allow more employees to get on, and then impatiently pushed the button for the lobby.

Merry arched her brows at her friend. He seemed to be in an almighty hurry.

As soon as the elevator hit the floor, Jayson shot out like he was being chased.

"Maybe he's got a hot date tonight," Lauren commented as they walked out of the building and toward the bus stop.

"Doubt it," Merry murmured. "I can't imagine any woman in her right mind being attracted to him."

CHAPTER FOUR

✳

Jayson

Jayson couldn't get out of the office fast enough. He'd enjoyed every minute he'd spent messaging with Merry this week. He had yet to even ask for her real name. For that matter, he hadn't divulged his full name, either.

Not important.

Not necessary.

He preferred she have no idea who he was. To Merry, he was just an overworked office employee not unlike herself. They'd exchanged a lot of personal information, including memories of their childhoods. He'd learned Merry lived with her parents and brother and that she worked in downtown Seattle, the same as he did. She was about as apple-pie as she could be, and he appreciated that. Her youth had been vastly different from his own. She'd had stability and love. Both she and her brother were cherished by their parents.

By contrast, Jayson had been used by his mother to manipulate his father. Precious little love had ever existed between them, and not near enough was left over to nurture him. He'd spent much of his childhood in boarding schools and summer camps with Cooper. For most of his childhood, when he was with family, he'd been shuffled around between his parents. Neither one wanted him. Neither one showed much interest in his emotional well-being. If it wasn't for caring teachers and a few good friends, he wondered what might have become of him.

His uncle, for whatever reason, had never married and had no children. All Matthew Matterson's energy had gone into building his consulting firm. He realized Jayson possessed the same drive and ambition, so he'd taken his nephew under his wing after college. Looking to prove his worth, Jayson had approached the job with an all-consuming passion that allowed him to climb to the position of vice president of the firm.

Merry was his first distraction in a long time. He should be thinking more about this contract with Boeing than spending time online chatting with her, but at this point his work hadn't suffered due to their budding relationship. He had to say, though, he found himself looking at the clock far more often than he ever had before, calculating how many hours it would be until they could chat again.

Speed-walking toward his condo building, Jayson stopped off at the Corner

Deli, where he collected a pastrami sandwich for his dinner along with a mixed green salad. He was a regular patron and was greeted by name by the owner.

"Hey, Jayson."

"Cyrus," Jayson responded, but he had no time for small talk.

Jayson walked past the woman ringing the bell for the red bucket, collecting for charity. He gave at the office. As he neared his condo, he noticed a homeless man had set up his bed for the night against the side of the building where Jayson lived. Much more of this and property values would be affected. Not good.

He pointed out the homeless guy to the doorman. "See what you can do about that," he instructed.

"Will do."

Peter, the evening doorman, was looking for a Christmas bonus. Jayson was one who appreciated excellent service and rewarded it generously. He was heading for the elevator that would take him to his condo when his phone pinged, indicating he had gotten a text.

While he waited, he reached for his phone. For one wild moment, he thought it might be Merry, then realized that would be impossible, as she didn't have his personal number. Only a select few did.

The text was from his father.

In town.

Jayson groaned. That meant Alex Bright was going to want to see him. Jayson had no desire to connect with him. He ignored the text and shoved his phone back into his suit jacket as the elevator arrived.

As he entered his condo, his phone rang. Irritated by now, he grabbed it and saw his father's face appear on the screen. Tightening his jaw, he was inclined to let the call go to voice mail. It would do no good, though. Knowing how persistent Alex could be, delaying the inevitable would serve no useful purpose.

"Yes," Jayson answered, revealing no warmth or welcome.

"Is that any way to speak to your father?"

"How long are you going to be in town?" he asked Alex, avoiding his father's remark. If it was up to him he would gladly cut off all ties with both parents. Unfortunately, that wasn't an option, because his uncle was his mother's brother, as well as his father's best friend. All he could do was maintain a safe distance from their toxic lives.

"I came to see you," his father insisted.

"I'm busy." Jayson made sure he was always busy when either parent was in town.

"How about dinner tonight?"

"I have a date." A slight exaggeration, as his date consisted of messaging Merry.

He was determined not to give up this one small pleasure because his father just happened to be in town.

"A date," his father repeated slowly. "That's wonderful. Bring her along."

"No thanks." If he did have an actual dinner date, no doubt his father would spend the entire evening flirting with her. No way. Not happening. The thought of Merry meeting his father made him cringe.

"You serious about this girl?"

Jayson hated these conversations. "Maybe." He was elusive, as that worked best with his father. The less either parent knew of his personal life, the better.

"It's time you thought about marriage," his father advised, as if Jayson would listen to any marital advice from the man who had sported four wives and an equal number of stepchildren, although Jayson was his only son.

"Perhaps," he replied, hoping that would satisfy his father.

"This girl you're seeing. Is she the one?"

It seemed Alex wasn't going to willingly drop the subject. "It's too early to tell."

"But you like her."

"I wouldn't be dating her if I didn't." He did like Merry. She interested him more than any woman he'd known to this point. The anonymity between them suited him and his purposes for now. One day they would meet, and most likely it'd be relatively soon. At this point, however, he was content with their messaging. Which reminded him . . .

Jayson glanced at his wrist. "I need to go."

"Not before we set a time to get together."

"Tomorrow." He would agree to just about anything if it meant he could get off the phone.

"Good. Dinner tomorrow. Don't disappoint me the way you have the last two times I've been in town."

Jayson had used several convenient excuses to get out of seeing his father. Meals with Alex could drag on for hours. Besides, it was highly probable that his father was romantically involved with some poor, unsuspecting woman who had no clue what she was getting herself into, and his dad usually brought her along. Jayson wanted no part of that.

This was a pattern. His father, showing his age now, would use younger women to boost his ego. In a sad attempt to prove what a fine catch he was, he would involve Jayson. Having a successful, handsome son was a credit to him.

"Make it lunch," Jayson suggested. "I have a date tomorrow night as well."

"Same girl?"

"Don't know yet."

He heard his father's sigh. "It's time to

stop playing the field, Jayson. Find the right woman and settle down."

This was an interesting tip, coming from his father.

"Yes. You're getting to the age when the right marriage to the right woman can be an asset to your career. Take my advice, find a woman who will look good on your arm and provide the right kind of business connections."

"I'll do that," he said, trying his best to hide his sarcasm. Then, unable to resist, he added, "Especially since marrying for money and connection has made you so happy and successful."

His father ignored the slight. "See you tomorrow."

Eager to get off the phone, he quickly agreed to a time and restaurant. Jayson ended the call without bidding his father farewell. Good riddance. He didn't know how long Alex Bright intended to stay in town. Hopefully it wouldn't be for long. Here today. Gone tomorrow. That was what he remembered about his father from his childhood.

Anxious now to get online with Merry, he went into his home office and logged on to the Mix & Mingle website and waited for Merry to do the same. In his rush, he'd left his dinner downstairs. He returned to the lobby to retrieve it, collecting a plate and fork in his kitchen along the way. He took everything into his home office with him.

As he began eating, he remembered seeing the data-entry temp eating her lunch at her desk and how it had annoyed him. He'd frowned upon the practice, and yet here he was doing the same thing. In retrospect, he should have commended her for being committed to her work. Too late now. The memo had already been issued. No eating at one's desk.

His computer dinged, indicating that Merry was online. Right away he started typing.

Wonder what it means that we're both home on a Friday night? he wrote.

Jayson thought about his dad in a downtown motel. Likely he was living it up, drinking too much and working hard to impress his latest conquest.

It says a lot, doesn't it? Merry typed.

Thing is, I wouldn't want to be anyplace else than right here, right now, chatting with you.

Are you sweet-talking me?

And if I was?

Then keep talking.

Jayson leaned back in his chair and smiled. He'd smiled more in the last week than he had in the last year, and it was all due to Merry. Involved as he was in this current work project, he hadn't realized how lonely he'd become.

Hope your day was good, Jay.

Kept looking at the clock, wondering how long it would be before we could chat. He wasn't sure he should admit this, but he did it anyway.

I did the same thing. My life is busy. I assumed there wasn't room for anything or anyone else, and then I connected with you, and, well . . .

Well what?

I'm not sure I should admit this.

Tell me.

My life is full and yet it's empty. I assumed all this time that I was content, but talking to you has proven that there's a part of me that hungers for an emotional connection. When I learned that Patrick and my mother had signed me up for Mix & Mingle, I brushed it off as something I didn't need or want. Messaging with you has opened my eyes.

Jayson read her note twice before he replied. Mine, too.

My friends are skeptical.

You mean because we haven't set a time to meet?

Yes.

Is that what you want?

He waited several moments for her reply as if she was mulling over her answer. It could be she was typing a lengthy reply, too.

Yes but not yet. Would you mind if we waited awhile longer? I'm finding just talking to you online is enough for now. It gives us both a chance to feel comfortable with each other.

Are you afraid meeting me will disappoint you?

Not at all. But I'd feel more comfortable about setting a time once I got to know more about you. It's more important to know who you are deep inside than what you look like. Besides, I have a small problem.

What kind of problem?

I'm working long hours now and have family obligations. And it's getting close to Christmas and I have a zillion things I need to do.

Like?

Baking. Mom, Patrick, and I bake for friends and family. It's our gift. Mom takes the baked goods to her friends whose MS is more advanced than her own. Then there's all the wonderful people in our lives who help us. Giving them something we've baked ourselves is our way of letting them know how grateful we are for what they do.

Service people?

Yes, but they're friends, too.

Like who?

There's a visiting home health aide who comes in and helps Mom two days a week, the postman, the newspaper boy, the teacher at Patrick's school. Those kinds of people.

In all his life, Jayson had never thought

to gift anyone other than his doorman, and he did that with cash. Totally impersonal. Easier for sure. Merry and her family gave of themselves. This was a completely foreign idea that left him wondering if this was something other families did.

Without Mix & Mingle, he would never have had the chance to meet someone like Merry. To be fair, he might have met her, but he wouldn't have given her a second thought. It made him aware of how narrow-minded he'd been when it came to his dating options, and what had been important to him in a woman.

He wanted to tell her about his father's visit and get her opinion.

Don't mind waiting to meet you. I'm busy with work, too. Plus, my father is in town. Not happy about that.

You don't get along with your father?

Not particularly. He didn't have much to do with me when I was younger and now he wants a relationship. Far as I'm concerned, I'm not interested.

Better late than never.

Thought you'd say that. From what he knew of Merry and her family, he wouldn't have expected anything less.

I love my dad.

He grinned, not surprised. You're lucky to have a decent father.

I agree. You might want to give your own dad another shot. Perhaps he's looking for a second chance with his son.

Don't think that will work.

It won't if you don't try.

I'll think about it.

From Merry's profile, Jayson knew she was in her mid-twenties. He had to wonder how it was that a woman this young could be so wise.

They typed back and forth for two hours. It was only when Merry had to leave to pick up her brother from his job at the Kroger grocery store that she needed to close. Otherwise, Jayson was convinced they could have continued into the wee hours of the morning.

After they'd logged off, he thought about what Merry had written about her father, who sacrificed and supported her family. Jayson considered his own father to be a failure on every level. He'd been a cheating husband; a piss-poor father; a shrewd, heartless businessman; and, for the most part, a lousy friend.

Jayson could count on his right hand the number of times his father had taken advantage of his visitation rights and spent time with Jayson. For all of Jayson's life, Alex Bright had considered his son a nuisance who was best ignored in the hopes that he would go away.

The following afternoon, father and son met in the dining room of the best steakhouse in town. Alex came alone, which was a surprise. Jayson noticed that his father had added on a few pounds around his middle, which told him the older man's lifestyle was catching up with him fast.

Alex Bright grinned and slapped Jayson across the back. "I'm glad you could squeeze me into your tight dating schedule."

Jayson slid into the plush steakhouse booth. "Like father, like son."

His father laughed and took the seat across from him. "So tell me, how is it you found time to meet me for lunch? I figured you'd cancel again."

That was the million-dollar question. Jayson released a long, slow sigh as he considered his answer.

"A friend said something that made me reconsider."

"A friend? What did he say?"

"She."

His father arched his brows. "What

did she say? Don't suppose it happens to be that girl you're dating."

Jayson preferred to leave the answer to speculation and ignored the question. "She said I should give you a chance. So, Dad, this is your chance."

Alex's eyes widened and, flustered now, he reached for the menu and avoided eye contact. "Thank her for me," he murmured.

Jayson stared at his father for a long time, not knowing what to think.

CHAPTER FIVE

✳

Merry

Merry spent the entire weekend decorating the house for Christmas. Shopping for the perfect Christmas tree had always been a family tradition. Patrick got so excited that once they reached the Christmas tree lot, he bounced from tree to tree like a jackrabbit, extolling the virtues of each one. Her brother simply loved the holiday season and was never happier than he was in the weeks leading up to Christmas morning.

It took hours to get the chosen tree home, up, and decorated. Christmas music

played in the background as they strung
the lights and added their special ornaments, many of which Patrick had made
over the years. There were more than a few
of her own. It was truly a Charlie Brown
tree except when it came to the ornaments,
but Merry loved that her mother had kept
them and insisted on using them year after
year.

On Sunday following church, Merry
and her mother baked cookies, and Patrick decorated the eggnog cookies with
frosting and sprinkles. While Merry was
busy placing the cutouts on the cookie
sheets, her thoughts drifted toward Jay.

During last night's chat, Jay shared that
he'd gone to lunch with his father, and
apparently their visit together had gone
relatively well. Not great. But better than
Jay had expected. It sounded like father
and son would never be "buddy-buddy,"
but they'd been able to have a decent conversation about each other's lives.

Merry had shared that she was going to spend Sunday afternoon baking cookies. Jay told her he couldn't remember the last time he'd tasted homemade cookies. Merry wanted in the worst way to give him a box and decided that when they met for the first time, she'd bring him a batch.

Monday morning, Merry arrived at the office thirty minutes early. Once there, she set up a tiny flower pot–size Christmas tree on the corner of her desk. Then she looped a silver garland around three sides of each office desk and hung glass ornaments strategically on each garland. When she finished, she stepped back to examine her work and felt good about what she'd accomplished. These few decorations added a bit of holiday cheer to their small department and brightened the area. They'd all been working extra-hard, putting in countless hours of over-time. This was her way of adding a little fun to their day and acknowledging the season.

Lauren was the first to arrive, and when she saw Merry's handiwork, her eyes lit up. "Cool."

"You like it?"

"Love it. I've been feeling down lately. It seems like I can't keep up with every-thing. This mandatory overtime is kill-ing me."

Kylie added her voice to Lauren's once she arrived. "Me, too." When she saw the decorations Merry had arranged around each of their desks, she clapped her hands. "This is great."

"I downloaded a few Christmas songs, too. Thought we could softly play those while we work."

"Super."

Kylie grinned. "I adore Christmas music."

"Just don't be tempted to sing along," Merry advised. "Someone might hear." By **someone**, she meant their annoying boss. Even a hint that they might be enjoying themselves was sure to upset him. It was all work, work, work for Bright. The man was a real Grinch.

"Mr. Bright," Kylie said, ending with a moan of displeasure.

"He doesn't know the meaning of the word **fun**." Merry struggled with negative feelings when it came to her boss. He looked like he was in a perpetual bad mood. His entire focus was on the business, as if this job was the meaning of life.

Merry knew this current project was important to the company and the reports had to be in before Christmas. She also understood that Mr. Bright held hope that if the report proved useful, the aircraft company would become a major client. Then Matterson Consulting would be able to expand and add more offices, and thus accumulate a higher profit. To Merry's way of thinking, bigger wasn't always better, but no one had sought out her opinion, least of all her boss.

They started work, typing in the data, listening to the Christmas carols as their fingers tapped against the computer keys. It was the best Monday Merry could remember having in weeks. Even knowing her workday would last for a long ten hours, her mood was good.

She thought about Jay and was eager to chat with him that evening. They hadn't been online nearly as long Sunday night as they had been earlier in the weekend because both had to be at work early on Monday. For her part Merry was tired from all the decorating and baking. Her weekend had been full of family activities.

Patrick seemed to realize how important Jay had become to his sister in this short amount of time. Her brother wanted to leave Jay a message, so she'd let him type a few lines to him on Sunday. It made her nervous wondering how Jay would respond to him. It pleased her with how patient he'd been with her brother to this point. He'd treated Patrick like he would anyone, and had been thoughtful and kind.

This alone comforted Merry in their growing relationship. Once, in high school, a date had made a joke about her brother, which had infuriated Merry. She never went out with him again, although he'd insisted it had all been in fun. Clearly, she couldn't take a joke, her date had told her. Jay had been wonderful, though, and that endeared him to her even more. After their Sunday night chat, she toyed with the idea of meeting Jay sooner rather than later. This evening when they went online, she was willing to approach him with the suggestion and see how he felt.

The afternoon was progressing smoothly until Mr. Bright happened to walk through their department. He paused when his gaze landed on the holiday decorations.

Merry looked up from her computer screen and glared at him, daring him to comment.

He regarded the three of them steadily before he asked, "Who did this?"

Merry stood ready to face him head-on. "Me."

"It's nice, but unfortunately, I have to ask you to take all this down."

"But why?" she asked, doing her best to hide her irritation. "It isn't disrupting our work. Ask Lauren and Kylie if you don't believe me. In fact, the music relaxes us so we work faster and more efficiently."

"I don't mean to—"

"What could you possibly have against Christmas?"

"I don't dislike Christmas," he insisted. "The employee manual clearly states—"

"The employee manual?" she repeated.

"It's required reading for all employees, Miss . . ." He paused and glanced at the nameplate on her desk. "Knight."

"I'm a temp and no one gave me an employee manual," she told him.

"Which explains why you were unaware of the rules. I can't let you keep these decorations up because that would encourage others to ignore company policy."

"I see," she said, biting into her lower lip. Far be it for anyone to enhance their work area or show a bit of cheer for the season.

As if reading her mind, Mr. Bright added, "The handbook specifically states there are to be no decorations for holidays. No displays on desks or floors. I apologize that HR didn't give you a handbook.

I'll see to it that you receive one. Please read it."

"I will," she murmured, although it was a little late, seeing that her last day working as a temp would be right before Christmas. Finding the time to read the manual, especially now, would be difficult.

"I suggest you start with page twenty, third paragraph from the bottom," Bright told her, as if knowing her intentions.

Naturally, he would know the handbook by chapter and verse.

"This has long been the company policy," he said defensively. "I didn't make the rules, Ms. Knight, but it is what it is. Can I count on you to remove these decorations?"

Merry expelled her breath and slowly nodded. "Yes."

"Thank you." He looked over her desk, and for one moment she was convinced he showed regret, but then she was probably mistaken.

"I'll make sure not to do it on company time," she assured him. "You should know I came in early and arranged all this before starting work."

"That's appreciated. Thank you."

He left then. The entire time they'd been talking, both Lauren and Kylie continued to work, doing their best to pretend not to notice their conversation.

Once he was out of sight, they stopped work and turned to Merry.

"You okay?" Lauren asked.

"Of course. I didn't know holiday decorations were against company policy," Merry said, biting the inside of her cheek. Her other team members apparently didn't, either, or they would have said something earlier.

"We'll help you take everything down," Kylie offered.

"No. It's fine," she assured her friends. "I was the one who put them up and I'll be the one to take them down." It took

Merry several minutes to settle her nerves. She didn't know what it was about their boss. It went without saying that he was under pressure. They all were. At times, it seemed he went out of his way to find fault with her. The truth was Merry thought Bright and the employee manual were all a bit ridiculous, yet she had the impression he hadn't been happy about asking her to remove the decorations. He'd simply been doing his job.

Thankfully, this was a temporary situation, and in a short time she'd have completed her contract with Matterson Consulting.

Once home, Merry's mother noticed her slumped shoulders. Or she may have noticed the way Merry closed the microwave door with more force than was necessary.

"Hard day, sweetie?"

"The worst," Merry said, whirling

around to face her mother. "Mr. Bright made me take down the holiday decorations and then at lunch I spilled tomato soup on my white blouse and if that wasn't bad enough I made a mistake and entered data in the wrong file and had to redo it all, wasting time when we're already on such a tight schedule."

Her mother, who was a salt-of-the-earth kind of person, frowned. "I'm sorry."

"Mom, you have nothing to be sorry about. This is all on me."

"Why would your boss make you remove the Christmas decorations?"

"Company policy," she reported, holding back a smile. "Page twenty of the employee handbook. Third paragraph from the bottom."

"Did your boss tell you that?"

"He did."

"It sounds like he wrote the handbook."

"I don't think so, although he must have the entire thing memorized." She wanted to blame Bright for her bad mood. It was easy to lay the fault on him, but she was the one who'd spilled her soup and the one who'd entered the data incorrectly. Still, it had all started with him.

Later that night, once she'd settled her nerves, Merry went online with Jay. Within only a few minutes he sensed something had upset her, and asked what was wrong.

I had a truly terrible, awful, no good Monday. Hope yours was better than mine.

Want to talk about it? I'm a good listener.

No, but thanks. If I reiterate everything that went wrong, that will only upset me again, and I don't want to waste another minute dwelling on the negative. Bottom line, I had a run-in with my boss. I'm over it and want to move on.

I hate the thought of you being upset.

Talking to you helps. And it did. Already Merry could feel her spirits rising. Chatting with Jay was exactly what she needed to help her deal with her horrible Monday.

I'd give anything to comfort you with a hug right now.

Merry hesitated. She'd give anything to get a hug from him. They'd decided to wait to meet, but maybe they were over-thinking this. If they waited too long it could become an issue.

Are you thinking what I'm thinking? she asked.

What keeps going through my mind is seeing you in person, talking face-to-face instead of through a computer, having coffee together, laughing together, reaching over to hold your hand . . . What do you say?

Although this was what she wanted, Merry hesitated. What made you change your mind?

I'm not entirely sure. Think it might be what happened this last weekend. Things changed between us.

She felt it, too. There had been a slight shift in their relationship, a deeper understanding. Jay had chatted with Patrick, and afterward it was as if she'd lowered a wall she didn't even know was there. He had, too. Their discussion, although shorter than usual, had grown deeper, more intimate.

I appreciated the advice you gave me regarding my dad. What you said made a difference. You helped me to see him in a different light. He seems to regret much of what's taken place in his life, the kind of father he's been. I had the feeling he's looking to make up for lost time. We'll never be bosom buddies, but I could talk to him without resentment and I thank you for that. After the lunch with my dad, I had the strongest desire to meet you. Are you ready for that?

You're serious? You want to meet?

I do, and the sooner the better.

It'll have to be next Sunday. I'm working

late every night this week, and Saturday I promised to go with Patrick and a group of his friends over to Leavenworth on the Christmas train. I won't be back until late.

Then Sunday it is. What time?

You're sure about this?

Positive. More so every minute.

How about three? I like the idea of us having coffee together.

After trading several messages back and forth, they decided on a meeting location: Starbucks in Pacific Place, a downtown mall. It was convenient to them both, although she'd need to take the bus. To be able to recognize each other, they agreed that he would wear a blue dress shirt and she would have on a beige coat with a brown-and-black plaid scarf.

Lauren and Kylie noticed Merry's upbeat mood first thing the following morning.

"Hey, what's up with you?" Lauren

asked. "Did you win the lottery or something?"

Merry could hardly contain her excitement. "Jay and I decided to meet this Sunday."

"Jay, that guy you met over the Internet?" Lauren asked, picking up on the conversation. "You do realize he could be a serial killer, right?"

"Would you stop?" Kylie teased. "This is the way women meet men these days. And who else could Merry mean? She's been loopy ever since she started messaging with this guy."

"Don't do it," Lauren advised. "Trust me, no good will come of this."

Merry suspected that was what her friend would say. "Don't worry, we're only having coffee."

"In a public place?"

"Yes, of course."

"This is so romantic," Kylie murmured

dreamily. "You know I'm living vicariously through you."

Lauren didn't agree. "You'll be disappointed. Mark my words."

"Lauren," Kylie chastised. "Don't say that. You need to let this play out."

Their coworker was having none of it. "Bet he's as ugly as sin and that's the reason he's waited this long to suggest you meet."

"Will you stop," Kylie said, and wagged her index finger at her coworker.

At this point, Jay's looks didn't matter to Merry. She enjoyed chatting with him, getting to know him. Over the last couple weeks, she'd discovered how much they had in common. While there was a lot about him that she didn't know, he'd opened a whole new world to her. They were kindred spirits, lonely souls, caught up in duty and commitment. It wasn't until they started talking that Merry realized how isolated she'd become. Her life consisted of home and work, with few social outlets.

That evening, when Merry logged on, Jay was waiting for her.

Well, did your coworkers talk you out of meeting me?

No. How did you know they would even try? His question was uncanny. It was almost as if he knew what Lauren had said. Did **your** friends try to talk you out of meeting me?

My friends are few and far between, Merry. My best friends live in other parts of the country. It's been all work and little play for me until I met you.

My dearest friend married a guy in the Navy and moved away. It's a lot of work and little play for me as well, which is why Mom and Patrick signed me up.

I'm grateful they did.

Me, too.

Patrick came into her room and sat down on the corner of her bed. "You talking to Jay?"

She sat crisscross style with her laptop balanced on her knees. "Yeah."

"Can I talk to him again, too?"

Seeing how patient Jay had been earlier, she let him.

Hi Jay. It's me. I'm Patrick. Sissy said I could type.

Did she tell you we're going on our first date?

Yes, and she said she was going to bring you cookies we baked as a surprise. I frosted them and put on the sprinkles, but there are more than eggnog cookies. You like cookies? I do.

I love cookies.

I like baking and eating. Sissy says she wants you back now.

K. Nice talking to you.

Merry rotated the laptop so she was in

control of the keyboard. Patrick had no idea he had ruined her small surprise and she wasn't about to tell him.

I'm back.

Cookies? Did someone mention cookies?

Well, you know what they say, don't you? The way to a man's heart is through his stomach.

The thing is, Merry, you won't need cookies to find your way there.

Merry read that line twice. It was too soon. He shouldn't be saying things like this. Too soon or not, she felt like she was walking two feet off the ground, happier than she could remember being in a long time.

Sunday couldn't come fast enough for Merry.

CHAPTER SIX

✳

Jayson

Sunday couldn't come fast enough for Jayson.

He was excited to finally have the chance to meet Merry. He didn't know the details of what had upset her at work this past week. She'd briefly mentioned her boss; the two apparently had a run-in earlier. Merry hadn't wanted to talk about it. He wished she would. Unfamiliar emotion rocked him and he was ready to punch whoever had upset her. He wasn't violent by any stretch of the imagination, and this overwhelming protective urge was foreign to him. Merry was a beautiful soul. Anyone who mistreated her should be made to regret it. His reaction told him how strong his attraction for her was.

The fact that Merry had been unwilling to discuss the negative gave him insight into her character. Merry wasn't one to linger on adversity. She wasn't looking for sympathy or reassurance. Whatever had happened, she'd handled it herself and didn't want to burden him or anyone else with her troubles. She did mention that she was tempted to not renew her contract with the company if they asked, but that was the extent of what she'd said. His admiration for her grew each day.

They'd chatted until almost midnight nearly every night. It was hard for them to stop talking. He'd had no idea he would have that much to say to anyone, let alone a woman he had yet to meet. She'd written about the Christmases of her youth and how her parents had worked hard to make them special, even with their limited finances.

The Christmases of Jayson's childhood had been hellish. There were always gifts—plenty of those for sure—but gifts meant little when only strife existed between the two most important people in his world: his parents. The one tradition his family had was heated battles, leaving him feeling unloved and unwanted.

The contrast between Merry's home life and his own was striking. Afterward he had a hard time sleeping, as his mind wandered and he imagined what Christmas would be like with Merry.

Naturally, there'd be a tall Christmas tree with handmade ornaments made by Patrick and their own children.

Wait.

Children?

Him with a family? No way.

The thought shook him to the point he sat up in bed. **What am I thinking?**

A couple weeks of chatting online with this girl and all at once he was walking through a field of daisies with a rainbow overhead and unicorns prancing close by. This wasn't like him.

Lying back down, he closed his eyes and tried to ease the tension from his limbs. As soon as he was half asleep once more, the same picturesque scene returned. The eight-foot Christmas tree filled the living room and the scent of freshly baked eggnog cookies stirred his senses to the point he could almost taste the frosting. Oddly, no gifts were under the tree in his daydream. Presents weren't the point, after all; besides, Santa had yet to arrive.

Santa?

Even as a young boy, Jayson had never believed in Santa. How could he? As far as he was concerned, he'd never had

a childhood. It wasn't that he was filled
with self-pity. Other children had it far
worse than he ever did. He'd always had
a place to sleep and food to fill his stomach. What he'd craved was love, and that
had been in shockingly short supply.

The following morning, Jayson made a
point of walking past Mary Knight's desk.
He'd felt bad about needing to ask her to
remove the decorations. It was a role he
disliked, but unfortunately it was necessary. He'd done his best to explain, and
he hoped she hadn't taken it personally.

As Jayson strolled past the data-entry
area, he noticed that the miniature
Christmas tree was gone as well as the
silver garlands around the cubicles. He'd
run into Mary before, he remembered,
when he'd found her eating at her desk.
The company had a perfectly decent
lunchroom, and he didn't like the idea of

Mary working through her lunch hour. He thought that perhaps she'd been in a rush to finish for the day because she had a date that night. That didn't set right with him, which was completely unreasonable. It made no sense that he should care. Mary was young and attractive, so there was every likelihood that she was romantically involved. Not that it was any of his business.

The fact was he liked Mary. She had a lot of spirit and wasn't afraid to share her opinions. He found himself thinking about her and instantly was filled with guilt. He was set to meet Merry soon and she was the one who held his interest.

He noticed Mary wasn't at her desk. Surprised, he checked his watch. He'd never known her to be late, and it was four minutes past eight. As the thought flittered through his mind, Mary came rushing toward her desk, carting a tray with three take-out cups. Apparently, this

was some fancy coffee drink for her team,
neither of whom had arrived yet, either.

Smiling and in a good mood, she
placed the cups on each of their desks
and hummed a Christmas carol as she
agilely moved from desk to desk. When
she glanced up, she must have caught
sight of him, because she paused, frozen
in place for several seconds, as if awaiting
his reprimand.

"We're allowed to drink at our desks,"
Mary reminded Jayson, as if he wasn't already aware of it. "I didn't see anything
in the employee manual that said otherwise."

"You actually read it?"

She hesitated. "Ah, no, but I will."

He smiled and she smiled back. Then,
feeling foolish at having been caught
watching her, he glanced at his wrist and
commented, "You're late."

Her smile disappeared. "Mr. Bright, if
you're looking for an excuse to fire me,

then all I ask is that you wait until just before Christmas."

The last thing he intended was for Mary to feel threatened. "Your position is secure, Ms. Knight."

"Thank you, but I realize it's only because you need me until this project is completed."

He opened his mouth to contradict her and stopped. This was getting awkward, and the last thing he wanted was to start his morning off with a verbal confrontation with a temp.

"I won't keep you any longer," he said, and headed toward his own office. Jayson felt uneasy with the way he'd handled the situation. He wished he knew what it was about Mary Knight that lingered in his mind.

Later that morning, when he was between meetings, Jayson's personal phone rang. He smiled when he saw Cooper's name come up on the caller ID.

"Hey, Jay," Cooper greeted in the same cheerful voice that was his signature. "What's going on?"

"Work, what else? What's on your mind?" He didn't have time for idle chatter. The project deadline was looming.

"Actually, Maddy wanted me to ask if you'll be bringing anyone with you to the wedding."

"The wedding isn't for months yet."

Cooper sighed, as if that was exactly the response he'd expected. "What can I say, the woman likes to plan ahead."

Jayson was about to tell him he would attend alone, but before the words could leave his mouth he hesitated. "I might."

"What?" Cooper sounded shocked. "I told Maddy I'd ask, but you've always been a lone ranger. You meet someone special since the last time we talked?"

"Yeah. Sort of."

"How do you 'sort of' meet someone?"

Jayson decided he might as well fess up, as Cooper would eventually find out anyway. "After you stopped by and told me about you and Maddy, I logged on to that website you mentioned."

"Mix & Mingle. Really?"

"Yeah, I know. I saw this photograph of a dog . . ."

"You're dating a dog?"

"No, Coop, I'm not dating a dog. And stop your snickering, I'm being serious."

"Okay, sorry."

"I saw the photograph and figured she was probably someone like me who wanted to be liked for herself."

"Are you telling me you signed up and messaged her?"

"Yup." He couldn't seem to wipe the grin off his face as he imagined the shocked look from his cousin.

"So, you haven't actually met face-to-face?"

"Not yet." He thought about their date for coffee on Sunday. "We've been talking online and I like her. A lot."

"Do you have any clue what she looks like?"

"Nope."

"That doesn't bother you?"

"Nope." It didn't. It really didn't.

"What if she's, you know, weird? For all you know you could be chatting with a fifty-year-old cougar."

Jayson barked a laugh. It had been easy for Cooper; he'd known Maddy from their childhood. "She is taking a risk same as I am. For all she knows, I could be a sixty-year-old pervert." That was what Merry's coworker had warned her; she'd shared that a week or so ago. He'd smiled when he read that and assured her she had no worries—he was exactly what he claimed to be. She'd believed him, and it sort of worried him that she would be so utterly trusting.

"You mean to say you didn't post your photo, either?"

"No, I put up one of Rocky."

"You didn't!"

He chuckled softly. "You wouldn't believe the 'winks' I got. But no one interested me more than this girl. She said her name is Merry, spelled M-E-R-R-Y. I figured she made it up, seeing how close it is to the holidays."

"Bro, listen, I'm glad to hear you've taken the leap. Just be careful. The fact she didn't put up a photo worries me."

"Why are you concerned? It's going to be great. I like this girl. I haven't felt this way about anyone." **Ever,** he added silently.

His cousin was uncharacteristically silent and then inquired, "So you're planning to meet soon, right?"

"Sunday afternoon. We're going out for coffee. Nothing big or elaborate. I realize we've only been talking for a couple weeks, but I should tell you, I'm hooked. I've never met anyone like her. She's level-headed, family-oriented, kind, and thoughtful." He closed his mouth before he said anything more. If this thing went south he didn't want to hand his cousin bullets to use against him.

"You do realize she could look like a dog, which is why she may have posted that photo in the first place."

Jayson had considered that. Still, it didn't matter. He was intrigued by her. **Her.** He thought about Merry almost continually. Their chats had become addictive. She made him smile, and when they said good-bye each night he felt warm and happy. Both feelings were foreign to him, and he hung on to that sensation for as long as possible after they ended their online chat.

"Bro. You still there?"

"Yes, sorry. I was thinking—"

"I hope this works out," Cooper said,

cutting him off. "And when the time comes, I'd like to meet this woman who's already got you twisted around her little finger."

"She doesn't," he countered, and couldn't decide who he was trying to convince—Cooper or himself.

Sunday afternoon Jayson was dressed and ready well before noon. In retrospect, he wished he hadn't told her to look for a man in a blue dress shirt. That was far too stuffy. He'd opted for that because it was his daily uniform and seemed a natural choice at the time. Merry must think he was a workaholic. That wasn't the impression he wanted to give her. He wished he'd said jeans and a sweater.

He smiled to himself, thinking that it would have been fun to buy one of those ridiculous holiday sweaters, like the one he recently saw in a store window, with battery-driven reindeer ears that flapped. Another one on display had a huge Santa face with a flashing light for the red nose. He was certain Merry would get a kick out of that.

By one o'clock, he was pacing in his condo, looking at his watch every few minutes. The closer the time came, the more anxious he felt.

Pacific Place was only a few blocks from his condo; less than a fifteen-minute walk. Unable to wait any longer, he left far too early and headed in that direction, taking a leisurely route. He passed a flower shop with a window display full of holly sprigs and potted poinsettias. For several minutes, he stared at the window and toyed with the idea of bringing Merry flowers. The temptation was strong and he wavered before finally giving in.

He wasn't a flower-giving kind of guy

and he wasn't sure what would be appropriate for her. Carting a potted poinsettia into Starbucks seemed ridiculous. Flowers would be a nice touch, though. Feeling self-conscious, he walked into the shop. He'd have been more comfortable in a Santa suit than he was in this place. To hide his nervousness, he stuffed his hands into his pants pockets and wandered around, seeking inspiration.

"Can I help you find something?" the salesgirl approached and asked.

Jayson hesitated. She looked like she might know a thing or two about situations such as his. Throwing caution to the wind, he mentioned his mission.

"I'm meeting a girl for the first time and was thinking it might be a nice gesture to bring her flowers."

"That's a wonderful idea. Someone you met online?"

He nodded, pleased that she understood the situation without him having to explain. "We've been chatting for a while, though."

"A bouquet of roses?" she suggested.

He shook his head instinctively, recognizing that roses were a little much. Merry was the kind of woman who enjoyed simple pleasures. He remembered how she'd once mentioned her affection for wildflowers. It was unlikely the shop carried flowers like that, but perhaps they had something close, so he asked.

"We recently got in a shipment of yellow daisies. Would those do?"

"Perfect."

The sales clerk wrapped them up beautifully and tied them together with a pretty silk ribbon. While Jayson felt silly walking into the busy shopping mall carrying yellow daisies, he couldn't wait to see Merry's face once she saw them.

He arrived early and was glad of it—otherwise he wouldn't have been able to snag a table. After standing in the fast-moving order line for two coffees, he took a seat so that he could keep an eye on the entrance.

Time crawled. Then three o'clock came and went.

At ten minutes past three, he grew restless. This didn't bode well. Being punctual himself, he usually found tardiness an irritation. Merry had never been late for their chatting sessions, well, other than the one time. Even then, her brother and mother had logged on and explained for her. If he'd been thinking, he would have given her his cell number. His mind raced with the possibilities of what might have gone wrong.

"Excuse me, are you going to need this chair?" a grandfatherly man asked.

"Yes, I'm waiting for someone."

The man thanked him and collected a chair from another table.

At three-thirty, Jayson decided not to

wait any longer. He was disappointed and worried. This wasn't like Merry.

As he made his way out of the Starbucks, he paused at the garbage dispenser and tossed the daisies into the can before he headed back to his condo.

CHAPTER SEVEN

*

Merry

Merry's mom, dad, and Patrick were anxiously waiting for her when she returned from her meeting with Jay. They were sitting in the family room with the fireplace going, writing Christmas cards while carols played softly in the background. Her mother wrote notes in each of the cards, and Patrick carefully wrote his name, leaving room for her dad and later for Merry to add their own signatures. This was the way they'd always done it. Every member of the family signed their own names.

"Merry, Merry, you're here," Patrick called out excitedly when he saw her. "Did you like Jay? Was he handsome and kind?" Patrick had been almost as excited about this meeting as Merry had been herself. Her brother leaped from his chair and rushed toward her, eagerly waiting for her to tell him everything.

Immediately, her mother sensed something was wrong. "Merry? Did something happen?"

"You look disappointed," her father added.

Defeated, Merry slumped onto the sofa, unable to find the words to explain. Wanting to hide her distress, she resisted burying her face in her hands. The entire bus ride home, her thoughts had been in utter turmoil. Even now she had a hard time accepting that Jay, the one who'd consumed her thoughts every day, was Jayson Bright, the boss she'd clashed with on more than one occasion. "I . . . I hardly know what to say."

"You met him, right?" her mother asked. "You obviously didn't spend a lot of time talking, seeing that you're back this soon."

She sadly shook her head. "I didn't introduce myself. In fact, I left without saying a word to him."

"You didn't even say hi?" Patrick frowned, as if he had a hard time understanding why she would ignore Jay.

"If you didn't introduce yourself, does that mean you left him there to wait?" Her mother was unable to hide her surprise and shared a look with her husband. "Merry Knight, that isn't like you."

"You didn't meet him, but you said you would," Patrick cried. Her brother glared at her as if he was the offended party. "You stood Jay up and that's mean. You did a rude thing, Sissy."

"I know." Her brother was right; walking away the way she had was cowardly of her. The shock of seeing Jayson Bright had thrown her off balance. Merry had been too stunned to do anything more than turn around and flee. All the way home she couldn't find a way to equate the man who insisted she remove the Christmas decorations from her desk with the charming, interesting guy she'd come to know online. The two didn't compute.

"Patrick, would you go watch TV in your room for a bit while I talk to your sister?" her mother asked.

He hesitated.

"Come on, buddy," her father encouraged, his arm around Patrick's shoulders. "Let's leave the women to sort this out."

"Okay," he agreed, "but you need to tell Merry she did wrong."

"I will."

"Good." Patrick returned his attention

to his sister. "I like Jay and I know he likes you, but he won't anymore because you were mean."

"I know." In retrospect, Merry felt dreadful about leaving Jay sitting in the coffee shop, waiting. She couldn't help wondering how long he'd remained before he realized she wasn't going to show. It made her heart ache.

Patrick hung his head. "Is he special like me? Is that why you didn't like him?"

"Oh Patrick, you know better than to ask me that. I'd like him even more if he was anything like you."

Her words seemed to appease her brother, who quietly left the room with his dad so Merry and her mother could talk.

"Tell me what happened," her mother said gently.

She didn't seem to be as upset with her as Patrick was. Merry looped a strand of hair around her ear. "Jay is Jayson Bright."

It took a moment for her words to sink in.

"Your boss?" Her mother's eyes rounded as soon as she understood the significance of what Merry was telling her. "The one who wouldn't let Kylie take care of her sick son?"

Merry nodded. "One and the same."

"The one who makes overtime mandatory?"

"Yup."

"Oh dear," Robin whispered on the tail end of a sigh. "But until you saw who he was, you liked Jay and enjoyed chatting with him."

"I did . . . I do." It wasn't like Merry could deny it. Jay had quickly become a large part of her world. She couldn't stop thinking of him. She counted the hours until they could connect, rushing home at the end of the work day. The man she saw at work wasn't the same man she'd

come to know online. And she wasn't
the same woman he knew from online,
either, and that was the crux of the problem. He would be just as shocked to dis-
cover the woman he had come to know
was the very one who clashed with him
at every turn. What she realized in those
fleeting moments before she'd turned
tail was that she was bound to be a huge
disappointment to him. He had someone else set up in his mind, and that
someone wasn't her. She couldn't bear to
see the look in his eyes when he realized he'd been chatting with the woman
whom he considered to be a major men-
ace at work.

"He brought along a bouquet of yellow
daisies," Merry whispered. It seemed impossible that Jayson Bright would bring
anyone flowers, let alone her. But then he
didn't know . . . just as she didn't know.

"You need to tell him, Merry," her

mother said in the same understanding voice she'd used earlier.

"Tell him it's me? No way, Mom. I can't. Let me finish this contract first. It goes to the end of the year, and if we finish this report for Boeing before Christmas, we've been told we can have the week between Christmas and New Year's off. My contract will be over then." She didn't mention that the employee handbook, which Jayson had insisted she read, clearly stated, "Dating between supervisors and their subordinates is strongly discouraged."

"Honey, I know, but you can't leave him hanging. You two have been talking for weeks. He must have been worried when you didn't show, wondering what had happened."

"If he finds out it's me . . . I can't. I just can't. Can you imagine how uncomfortable it would be for us? I mean, the two of us working together. He might even think I somehow arranged all this, tricking him. I know it sounds crazy. All the way home these different scenarios kept going through my head of what Jayson Bright would say had I walked through those doors to meet him." She briefly closed her eyes, trying to imagine the scene, the big reveal. She couldn't see how any good would come from it.

"Merry, you know as well as I do that honesty is the best policy," her mother reminded her. "I'm sure Jay would be as shocked as you, but he'd get over it soon enough. Given time, I believe he'd accept you for who you are, for the woman he's come to know. But by your action today, you've taken the option away from him."

While Merry would like to think that it wouldn't matter who she was, the risk was too great. "I don't want to take the chance . . . remember, he's a stickler for the rules and practically has that employee manual memorized. The company has a clear policy about employees fraternizing." There was a lot at stake in this, especially her heart. She was half in love with Jay already. The problem was she couldn't reconcile that her boss was Jay. Her Jay.

"No matter what you decide, you owe it to Jay or Jayson to tell him the truth," her mother said, and hesitated as though unsure. "If nothing else, you should explain why you didn't introduce yourself."

"Maybe." Merry hadn't concluded in her own mind how best to resolve this problem. Patrick was right, though. Leaving without offering an explanation had been rude. In retrospect, she should have sent someone over with a message to tell him she wouldn't be coming.

"Merry," her mother said pointedly. "Do whatever it is you do and get online and talk to him. He needs to know you're safe. Explain as best you can. You owe Jay that much."

"Okay, okay." She wasn't happy about it, but she knew her mother and Patrick were right. She owed Jay an explanation, though she didn't know what she could possibly tell him to excuse her behavior.

Once in her bedroom, she climbed onto her bed and scooted up so her back was braced against the headboard. With her laptop resting on her legs, she assumed her usual position. It was the same way she sat every night when "talking" to Jay.

As soon as she logged on, Jay was waiting. His words flashed up on the screen.

What happened? Why didn't you show? Are you all right?

I could be better.

Her cursor flashed at her for several seconds. Before she could type, Jay's next words popped up on the screen.

You're sick?

No. I was there.

You were there?

Yes . . . and I decided against introducing myself.

Again, the cursor repeatedly flashed, blaming her.

Can you tell me why?

It's complicated.

Uncomplicate.

Jay was angry and she couldn't blame him. His one-word response said as much.

I wish I could. I'm sorry, Jay, but the minute I saw you I realized it would never work between us. We're too different . . .

Don't tell me that. It's an excuse. A lie. We've talked every night for weeks and have connected on a dozen different levels. It's something else, isn't it? Something you're unwilling to tell me.

No need denying it.

Yes.

What is it? You owe me that.

Please don't ask. Just accept that a relationship between us isn't a good idea. It's better to accept that now and move on. I'm sure there are any number of women on Mix & Mingle who would be a better match for you than me.

There was that dreaded cursor again, flashing accusingly at her.

Just like that? You're willing to give up on us without giving me a single reason? Unbelievable. How could I have spent all these nights talking to you and not know you? This doesn't make sense. I can't believe you're doing this. I brought you flowers. Not once in my entire life have I given a woman flowers.

Yellow daisies.

You saw and still you refused to meet me. That says it all. I should have known better. Lesson learned. My bad.

I'm sorry.

Jay didn't reply and logged off.

For a long time afterward, Merry sat on her bed, feeling numb and sick at heart.

Patrick knocked on her bedroom door.

"It's okay, Patrick, you can come in."

Her brother stuck his head past the door and stared at her for a long moment. "Are you sad?"

Merry nodded. "Yeah." **Sad** was a good word for the way she felt. **Disappointed, discouraged,** and **upset** were also part of the emotions taking up residence in her heart. She patted the edge of her bed, urging her brother to come join her. She closed her laptop and set it aside as Patrick climbed onto the mattress and sat down beside her.

Merry wrapped her arm around his shoulders and leaned her head against his, and he said, "I'm sad, too. I liked Jay. He was nice."

"He was nice," Merry agreed. "Sometimes people aren't right for each other, and I could see that I wasn't the right person for Jay."

"That's what makes you sad?"

"Yes, real sad."

Patrick released a deep sigh. "Are you going to look at some of the other men on the website to date them?" he asked.

"Maybe."

Her brother was silent for a couple moments. "That's what Mom says when she means **no** but she doesn't want to say **no**."

Merry grinned. Her brother was smarter than she gave him credit for. The sick feeling in the pit of her stomach was sure to last a long time. She had no desire to start an online relationship with anyone else. "I might look at other possibilities, but it won't be soon."

"Can I help you pick him out?"

"Sure." Seeing that she had a six-month subscription, Merry had plenty of time to decide. Presently, her inclination was never to go on the website again.

———

On Monday morning, Merry walked into the office to find both her friends watching and waiting for her.

"So?" Kylie asked, venturing first. "How'd the meeting go with your handsome Prince Charming?"

Merry had thought long and hard about whether she should update her friends with the truth or not. In the end, she decided it was better that they not know her Jay was Jayson Bright, their boss.

"Well?" Lauren prompted, when Merry hesitated. "I was right, wasn't I? He's a sixty-year-old pervert."

Merry took her time removing her coat and tucking away her purse. "He isn't sixty and he isn't a pervert."

"What happened?"

She shrugged. "It didn't work out."

"Told you," Lauren said, crossing her arms. "These online dating services never do."

"Oh stop," Kylie flared. "What went wrong?"

Merry shrugged. "He just wasn't what I expected."

"What did you expect?" Kylie asked, grinning. "A Saudi prince?"

Despite herself, Merry smiled. "I guess in some ways I did, but he's not even close to royalty."

"Told you."

"Lauren!" Kylie snapped. "Enough." She returned her attention to Merry. "You're disappointed, aren't you?"

"Terribly." It was the truth. Merry was more let down than words could possibly say. She held back a yawn. She'd tossed and turned most of the night and probably had only a couple hours of uninterrupted rest. All night her mind kept going to a nightmare in which she came face-to-face with Jayson Bright. In her dream, he was as shocked and as dismayed as she'd been.

And that was the crux of the matter. She liked Jay. She was half in love with Jay. But Jayson? Not so much. And yet they were the same person. She had yet to understand how that could be possible.

Somehow Merry made it until the end of the day. As she finished and was about to head home, she happened to look up in time to see Jayson Bright walking toward the elevator.

One of the staff from another department wasn't watching where she was walking and bumped into him. Merry held her breath, waiting for him to get upset. It was what she had come to expect from him. Instead, Jayson gripped hold of the older woman's shoulders so she didn't lose her balance and then bent down and helped her gather the papers that had fallen to the floor.

When he'd finished, he started toward the elevator, his shoulders slightly hunched. Merry couldn't take her eyes off

him. He looked as sad and beaten down
as she felt, which left her to wonder . . .

Had she made the right decision?

Was this what she really wanted?

And why, oh why, did the night ahead
feel so empty?

CHAPTER EIGHT

Jayson

Thursday evening arrived, and it'd been four days since Jayson had last spoken to Merry. Over the first couple days, anger had consumed him. He'd been a fool to have anything to do with that website. With her. This whole idea of dating someone he'd never met had been crazy. **What was I thinking?** Merry had played him for a fool. He'd never needed a dating service in the past. As far as he was concerned, Mix & Mingle had been one colossal mistake, and one he had no desire to repeat.

However, as the week progressed his anger mellowed. Bored and restless, he logged on to the site, wondering if Merry had left him a message. An explanation. Anything. He'd had several other winks but none that interested him. He wanted Merry.

When he looked, he found a message waiting for him.

From Merry.

His heart rate accelerated, and he blinked to be sure he wasn't imagining it. To be sure, he opened the message.

Only Merry wasn't the one who'd written him.

The note was from Patrick.

My sister is sad. She likes you a lot.

Interesting. Jayson was tempted to ignore it, but then on a whim decided to leave a message of his own.

She didn't want to meet me, Patrick. I wanted to meet her in the worst way. Can

I ask you a question? Can we talk in an hour?

Jayson didn't know if Patrick would see his note, but it was worth a shot. Merry's brother must have been at the computer, because he answered right away.

I do homework then.

Can we talk now? he asked. With Patrick's help, Jayson might have a chance of learning what had happened.

Okay, but I can't talk more than an hour.

That was fine by him. Great. I'm sad, too, Patrick, because I like your sister. Finding out what she'd found so objectionable about him had almost become an obsession. He couldn't go more than an hour or two without thinking about her. What was worse was not knowing. Perhaps she was someone he'd dated in the past or someone related to a former girlfriend. The possibilities were endless.

Merry's rejection had been a bitter pill

to swallow. As the days had passed, he found it harder and harder to accept her decision. That left him one option, and that was to find her and ask her face-to-face. He couldn't imagine anything worthy of the way she'd dumped him with no explanation or excuse.

I knew you would want to see her. Merry is pretty, but she doesn't date a lot.

I'll make her smile again.

She needs to smile. It's Christmas and she shouldn't be sad.

You're right, she shouldn't.

Patrick added, Don't tell her I talked to you because she might not like me doing that.

I won't say a word.

Promise?

I promise. Time to get to the nitty gritty. Can you tell me what her real name is? He was certain Merry was a name she used because she didn't want him to know her actual given name.

Patrick stopped typing as if he didn't understand the question. That's funny. Her name is Merry. You know that.

That's her real name?

That's what we call her. I don't think she has another name. Her middle name is Noelle.

Okay. Interesting. He'd go about this in a different way. What's your surname?

Is this a test? I don't do good on tests.

No test.

I need help. Patrick typed. What's a surname?

Your last name.

I know this. But I'm not supposed to tell strangers.

Jayson groaned. The only thing he could figure was that it had been pounded into Patrick not to give out his name to people his family didn't know.

Where does Merry work?

Downtown.

Jayson groaned again. Getting information out of her brother was proving more challenging than he'd hoped.

Do you know the name of the company where she works?

Yes. I need to think.

He prodded when Patrick didn't answer for several pulsing seconds. Think. It felt like a month before the youth typed in his response.

I didn't remember, so I asked her, but she told me that work is work and home is home. Don't worry, I didn't tell her I was talking to you.

Good. I want to find Merry and talk to her.

I know she takes the number-eighteen bus to work. Sometimes I meet her at the bus stop, but only in the summer, because it's dark out in the winter.

That's a nice thing to do.

She likes it. I need to go now. Mom is calling me.

Thank you for your help, Patrick.

I did good on the test, right?

Very good. Bye for now.

He was about to close his computer when another message popped up. This time it was Merry.

Are you drilling my brother with questions about me?

No need denying it, he'd been caught red-handed. Yes.

Don't. Please. It's not fair to use my brother for your selfish purposes.

Perhaps not.

Don't you care?

I'm not willing to give up on us, Merry. He says that's your real name, by the way.

It is.

And Smith is your surname?

I'm not answering that.

Figured you wouldn't. It appears you have a December birthday, Merry Noelle Smith.

Not answering that, either.

Merry might not be answering his

questions, but she was talking to him, and that was all that mattered.

I miss you. I can't believe you don't miss talking to me. Be honest, Merry. Give me that.

All right, if you must know . . . yes, I miss you, too.

Then tell me what it is you find so offensive about me that makes you refuse to meet me.

The cursor blinked for several uncomfortable seconds while he awaited her reply.

I know you.

That made Jayson sit up and take notice. You know me? How?

I need to end this. All I ask is that you don't talk to my brother again.

Don't go. He swallowed his pride, and in a desperate note added, Please.

Merry didn't sign off, and he sighed with relief.

Was I rude? Unreasonable?

I'm one of the little people you choose to ignore. That's all I'm willing to tell you. As soon as I saw who you were, I realized that the man I've come to know online is a different person than the one I've met previously. I can't find a way to connect the two.

Jayson didn't know what to tell her.

I accept that I can be rude and impatient. I'm working on it.

Maybe you should work harder.

Jayson grinned. She wasn't holding back.

Will you chat with me again?

Her answer took a long time coming, but he waited, working on his patience.

I don't think that's a good idea.

He wasn't willing to accept that. Nine tomorrow night. He didn't wait for her to reply. As the saying goes, the ball was in her court now.

———

Friday afternoon, just as he was about to leave the office, Jayson got the last piece of information needed to finalize the report for Boeing. This was what he'd been waiting weeks to receive. The data would need to be entered, and he didn't want to wait until Monday morning before submitting his conclusion. Christmas was right around the corner, and his hope was to get this report into the proper hands ahead of schedule.

The mandatory overtime had ended, but he wanted this done pronto so he could review it over the weekend. He might as well work. That would keep his mind occupied until he could sort out this mess with Merry.

He was no closer to tracking her down now, although he felt encouraged. His chat with Patrick had given him a few clues, but not enough to figure out her identity. She claimed she was one of the little people. His first thought was that she worked in the service industry. Perhaps she was the barista who routinely made his morning coffee. He hoped not. From what he saw of her, she wasn't especially bright. The woman who came to clean his condo once a week was a grandmother. Perhaps Merry was someone related to her. It might even be someone in the office, but he couldn't imagine who. The little people? What did she mean by that? A housekeeper? A server? A receptionist?

He stopped off at the Corner Deli a few nights each week, so perhaps Merry worked with Cyrus. His mind mulled over the options. She could be someone he routinely saw and had never noticed.

He pulled his thoughts away from Merry and back to the project and what needed to be done. Leaving his office, he walked down to the data-entry department to find the three women diligently working.

Mary was the first one to look up, and she blinked as though shocked to see him. They'd had their minor disagreements, and Jayson regretted that. When Jayson had called HR to learn more about her, he was told that Mary was contracted for a year and had filled in for the head of the department, who had given birth to twins and requested twelve months' leave. According to what he'd learned about her, she had done a fantastic job, but the position would end at the first of the year, as the woman she replaced would return then.

Mary stopped typing, and soon the other two women followed suit. All three of them looked at him, apparently waiting for him to say something.

"I need someone to stay this evening," he said. "It will probably require a couple hours." Then, remembering his determination to be less demanding and more patient, he added, "Mary, as the head of the department, I'd like you to decide who should work the overtime."

The woman with the nameplate that said LAUREN spoke first, looking at Mary. "Sorry, I can't stay. I've got family arriving this evening from Kansas. I agreed to pick them up at the airport. They're here for the holidays."

The second woman spoke up. "Billy has his school Christmas program this evening." Her eyes were apologetic. "I can't miss that. Billy plays the role of the little drummer boy."

Mary sighed and turned to her boss. "Guess you're stuck with me."

"Will this be a problem?" he asked.

"It's Friday night and . . ."

"I realize working overtime is probably ruining your date night," he snapped, and then instantly regretted his outburst. Drawing in a calming breath, he tried again. "I would appreciate your help."

She didn't correct him, which led Jayson to realize he'd guessed right. She did have a date.

"I'll need to make a phone call."

"Thank you. I have the necessary paperwork in my office. I'll be right back."

When he returned, Mary was alone, as the other women had left for the weekend.

He handed her the report. "I want you to know I appreciate your willingness to do this."

She offered him a brief smile and a dimple appeared, just one on the right side of her mouth. This wasn't the first time he'd noticed it. The dimple mesmerized him. She seemed to realize he was staring at her, which flustered him. To cover his discomfort, Jayson pulled up a chair and sat down before spreading out a large sheet with the necessary statistics listed.

CHAPTER NINE

✳

Merry

They worked together, side by side, and with every moment Merry grew more aware of the man sitting next to her. Jayson gave her the necessary information and Merry entered it into the computer. She tried to do her best to keep her mind on track. She'd never been this close to Jayson before, and had never noticed the spicy scent of his cologne. It swamped her senses as she breathed it in. About ninety minutes later, when they were halfway through the report, Merry needed a break.

She'd made a few mistakes, something she rarely did. Being this close to Jayson distracted her. When he paused, she straightened and rubbed her hand along the back of her neck.

Jayson noticed and set the papers down. "Let's take a ten-minute breather."

"Good idea." She stood and stretched. Determined to take a mental break, she made an excuse and headed to the ladies' room. When she returned, Jayson was nowhere in sight.

What? Maybe he thought it would be best if she finished on her own? Merry felt an immediate sense of loss. **Well, so be it,** she thought. Feeling let down, she started again on her own.

Being alone left her feeling bereft. This was the first time it'd been just the two of them. These ninety minutes had given her insight into Jayson that she wasn't able to see through their online exchanges. He'd been patient, especially when she'd flubbed up the numbers, transposing them. Thankfully, he'd caught her mistake. Thoughtful, too. She hadn't said out loud that her neck ached and that she needed a break. He saw her rub her hand along her neck and recognized that she could use a few minutes to relax her shoulders.

With him gone, she glanced around the deserted office and noticed all the other areas were darkened. The office had never appeared so stark or bare. It hadn't felt like that when Jayson was by her side.

She took note of the time, and the thought went through her head that he needed to be home before nine so they could chat online, though she supposed he could use his work computer. There was plenty of time still. The irony didn't escape her. Jayson assumed she'd canceled or delayed her Friday-night date, not realizing, of course, that her date was with him.

Yes, against her better judgment, she'd decided to chat again with Jay that evening.

She'd regretted giving in at the time. Now she wasn't so sure, seeing this new side of him. He was much more her online Jay tonight than Jayson, her rude and sometimes dictatorial boss. The problem was how she would go about letting him know who she was. But not yet. It was still too early to make that decision, but if she believed they had a chance, she would.

This relationship was important to her. When she'd admitted that she'd missed their time together online, it hadn't been an exaggeration. She'd felt as if she'd been at loose ends all week, and if she was being honest, she'd been miserable. Even Patrick had noticed, which was what had prompted him to reach out to Jay without her approval.

Merry had found Patrick sitting at the computer, intently typing away. When he noticed her watching, the guilty look on his face was all she needed to guess what he'd been doing, and she'd confronted him. Her brother was as readable as a dinner menu.

Poor Patrick's face instantly went bright red, knowing he'd been caught. He'd immediately blurted out that he'd been chatting online with Jay.

"Why would you do that?" Merry demanded.

"You were so sad, and I knew Jay was sad, too, and so I had to tell him." Her brother lowered his head and Merry couldn't argue—her brother was right.

At first Merry had been upset. Not with Patrick but with Jay. When she'd realized he was still online, her fingers had pounded on the computer keys, unable to hide her irritation. Her anger hadn't lasted long, though. She'd missed him. So much.

And he'd missed her.

Then he'd typed that one word. The one that convinced her to continue.

Please.

She couldn't refuse him, couldn't refuse herself. Later that night, her emotions were mixed and she wavered back and forth, wondering if she'd done the right thing.

Footsteps echoed in the office and Merry stopped typing, alert now because she wasn't alone. A shadowy figure appeared. It didn't take her long to recognize that it was Jayson.

He'd come back.

He held two take-out drinks in his hand. Before she could say anything, he set one on her desk.

"I didn't know where you were," she blurted, and immediately regretted it.

He blinked, seeming surprised that she'd care. "Guess I should have left a note."

"It was creepy here by myself." That sounded better than admitting how keenly she'd felt his absence.

"Sorry, Mary, that was thoughtless of me. I assumed I'd be back in only a few minutes, but the line at Starbucks was long. Apparently, something's going on downtown tonight. I heard several people mention something having to do with Figgy Pudding, whatever that means."

He smiled and her heart melted. "Oh . . . it's a singing choral contest that benefits the local food banks," she blurted, the words spilling out of her.

"That explains it," he said, and then, looking down at the drink in his hand, he added, "I got you an eggnog latte. I thought you might need something to tide you over."

She blinked, surprised by his thoughtfulness, and she was grateful. "Ah . . . thanks."

"I hope you like eggnog."

"I do." It was her favorite for this time of year.

He grinned and all she could do was stare. Jayson Bright's entire face was transformed by a simple smile. His eyes brightened as their gazes connected. Fearing she was about to reveal herself, Merry made a determined effort to look away, although she immediately felt a sense of loss.

"You like Christmas, don't you?" he asked.

Merry sipped her latte and nodded. "It's my favorite time of year."

From their weeks of lengthy conversations, she knew Jayson's childhood had been less than nurturing. He'd told her about his parents' unhappy marriages and his life in East Coast boarding schools.

There had been almost a complete lack of tenderness in his life.

What Jayson saw in her, the online Merry, what attracted him to her, she suspected, went back to his childhood. Whether he recognized it or not, Jayson was drawn to the warmth and love of family.

Her family.

That sense of belonging was the real draw. In terminating their relationship, claiming there was no hope for them, she'd taken that warmth and acceptance away from him. The stories she'd shared with him about their holiday traditions— decorating the tree, baking cookies, sending out Christmas cards—had been like a drug to someone who had never known what it meant to be part of a family. Little wonder he was willing to let go of his pride and plead to continue their online relationship.

Jayson cleared his throat, distracting her from her thoughts.

"You're staring at me."

"I am. Sorry," she murmured, embarrassed, looking away. Because she felt she needed to offer an excuse, she said, "It's just that I didn't expect the latte. Do I owe you anything?"

"No, Mary, I'm the one who owes you. You don't need to reimburse me."

She took the Starbucks cup and set it aside. "I started again and got quite a bit done," she said, eager to get back to inputting the data.

Jayson grabbed the chair and scooted next to her desk, papers in one hand and coffee in the other.

It was close to eight by the time they finished.

"I couldn't have done it without you, Mary."

"I was happy to help," she said, and she meant it.

"I'm thankful for your time," he said, moving back his chair.

She reached for her coat and purse and noticed he remained seated, reading over the last of the report.

"You're staying?" she asked, wondering how late he would remain at the office. As for herself, she needed to hurry if she was going to catch the eight-fifteen bus, otherwise she'd be late to chat with . . . him.

"No, I need to get home myself." He stood and headed toward his office. "Give me a minute and I'll walk you out."

"Oh." That was another surprise. Jayson Bright was turning into a man she barely recognized. The two Jays were merging together in her mind and she wasn't sure that was a good thing. It would make keeping her true identity a secret that much more complicated.

Once he'd locked up the office, they walked to the elevator and stepped inside.

"Have you ever noticed," he asked, suppressing a smile, "how the reflection shows in the smooth surface of the elevator door?"

What an odd question. "Not really."

His mouth quirked again.

"What makes you ask?" As soon as she phrased the question, Merry knew the answer.

"If you're going to make faces at me behind my back, Mary, you might want to make certain that your reflection doesn't show on the doors."

She gasped and was convinced her face turned the color of an overripe tomato. Once she found her voice, she said, "It's a wonder you didn't fire me."

"The thought never entered my mind."

"I'm sorry; that wasn't professional of me."

"No worries. I was more amused than upset."

The elevator landed on the ground floor and they walked together toward the exit.

"Your Friday-night date—was he upset about you needing to cancel?"

"No, it worked out fine. We aren't getting together until later anyway," she assured him. What he didn't know was that her hot date was a conversation . . . later, at nine, with **him.**

He checked his watch. "What time is he picking you up?"

She didn't dare explain that there would be no "picking her up" for her date, who unknowingly stood by her side. "Nine."

She turned and rushed toward the bus terminal, walking at a clipped pace along the brightly lit avenue. The trees were strung with white lights, giving a festive air to the cold night. Merry was surprised when Jayson's steps caught up to hers.

"You don't have a car?" he asked.

"I ride the bus."

"In that case, I'll drive you."

He glanced at his watch. Merry knew with the Seattle traffic being what it was, he'd never return in time. If he did, he'd be late for their date. That he would offer to drive her home, knowing he would be late, was completely unexpected.

She wanted to talk to Jay; she'd been looking forward to it all day. "I appreciate the offer, but it's not necessary."

"I don't want you to be late for your date."

"I won't be. The bus is the most efficient way for me to get home."

He hesitated and she secretly wanted to tease him for being so willing to give up his "date" with her. Of course, he didn't know that.

"If you're sure."

"I'm sure."

He walked her to the bus stop, and they went their separate ways.

Merry was home, sitting in front of her computer, at nine. Jay didn't leave her waiting long.

Merry? Is this you, or is this Patrick again?

She didn't understand why he would ask her that, then remembered that she hadn't agreed to go online.

It's me, Merry.

If you could see me, you'd see a big smile. I wasn't sure you'd be online.

The truth is I couldn't stay away.

I couldn't, either. I want you to know I've given a lot of thought to what you said to me. You're right. I'm arrogant and annoying, but I'm trying not to be. I'm willing to change my ways if that means I can have a chance with you.

Merry had already seen the evidence of that, although she couldn't let Jayson know.

This evening I went out of my way to be nice to one of the office staff.

A woman? Should I be jealous?

Maybe.

Merry grinned. Little did he realize she was the employee he was referring to.

You better explain.

I asked her to stay late and she did.

I hope you paid her double time.

She's a temp, but yes, I'll be sure she's well compensated. Later I offered to drive her home.

This was the perfect opportunity to find out what Jayson thought of her. If they ever did meet, he might not take kindly to the underhanded method she'd used, but so be it. The temptation was too hard to resist.

Is she young? Single?

Yes, to both.

Hmm, interesting. Is she pretty?

Pretty enough.

Pretty enough! Merry was insulted. Fingers at the ready, she was about to tell him exactly what she thought of his assessment of her. Thankfully, she stopped before she gave herself away.

You're taking a long time to respond. You're jealous, aren't you?

A little. She decided to humor him.

No need. You're the one who fills my head. Besides, she's involved with someone else. Had a date she was hurrying home to meet. It's you, Merry. You. You're the one who has talons in my heart.

That sounds painful.

It is. If only you knew. Tell me you're willing to meet me. Let's put this silliness behind us.

She was tempted. Really tempted. Not yet.

If not now, when? He sounded frustrated with her.

I'm not sure. It'll happen when the time is right.

She could almost feel his frustration. All right, I'll prove I can be as patient as the next man. I'm grateful you're willing to talk to me again.

A full two hours passed with them exchanging messages. The time flew by, and when she was finished, a warm, happy feeling came over her. She didn't know how she was ever going to find the strength to let go of Jay.

This chatting isn't enough for me any longer. I want to get to know the flesh-and-blood Merry. Please reconsider.

His "please" got to her every time. It told Merry she was as important to him as he was to her, and that denying him would be almost impossible.

Okay, I give in. We'll meet before this year ends.

Promise?

Promise.

Merry didn't know what would happen when he learned who she was. One thing she did know was that she couldn't bear it if he broke her heart, because he already held it in the palm of his hand.

CHAPTER TEN

Jayson

Jayson worked the entire weekend, finishing the report that he would present on Tuesday to the Boeing executives. He'd been analyzing the data for weeks but was only now able to draw a conclusion. He was pleased with the results and convinced his insights would save the company money without requiring layoffs. It felt good that he could offer a viable solution to their current needs.

The only breaks he took over the entire weekend had been to chat with Merry. Spending time with her, even if it was online, was like taking a summer stroll. It refreshed and invigorated him. After they talked, he felt ready to tackle the project again with renewed energy and insight. He didn't know what it was about her that inspired him. All he knew was how he felt. He wasn't a man driven by feelings. He'd never been comfortable with them. As a youth, he'd learned to suppress and hide his emotions. Merry had the ability to draw them out unlike anyone he'd ever met. The guard he kept between himself and others had disappeared behind the anonymity of the computer screen.

By Monday morning, he was both exhausted and exhilarated. He'd met his deadline and was eager to have his uncle read his conclusion. As he entered the building, his gaze instinctively went toward the data-entry department.

Mary had been instrumental in helping him with the final phase of the report. He saw that she was at her desk and decided to stop by and thank her once again. Merry had questioned him about Mary on one of their weekend chats, and he'd made light of his interest in her. He had strong, strange feelings for Merry, but she seemed to be secretive and wary, which raised questions in his mind.

What surprised Jayson was that he found himself attracted to Mary, too. Over the weekend, he'd found his thoughts drifting toward her and he had to forcibly turn his mind away from her. He wasn't sure what it was about her.

When Mary noticed him, she looked up and automatically smiled. Over the last few weeks he'd caught her frowning at him any number of times. Seeing her welcoming smile now caught him off guard. His steps slowed as he worried that he was flirting with temptation.

"Good morning," Mary said, her eyes bright and welcoming.

"Morning."

"Did you finish the report?"

He didn't remember mentioning it to her, but clearly he must have. "I did, and I wouldn't have been able to if you hadn't stayed on Friday."

"I was happy to do it."

"I wanted to be sure you knew how much I appreciated your help."

"You're welcome, Mr. Bright."

He grinned. "No need to be formal. My name is Jayson."

Her eyes twinkled when she asked, "Is that allowed in the employee handbook?"

Chuckling, he said, "It's all right to make an exception now and again."

"Good to know."

As he started toward his office, he noticed a couple people giving him odd looks, and he wondered if it had anything to do with the smile on his face.

Mary amused him. He found it interesting how one night of working late together could change their testy relationship. He wasn't sure what exactly had brought about the transition; whatever it was, it pleased him.

First on his agenda Wednesday morning was the meeting with his uncle, who praised him for getting the report finished ahead of schedule. Jayson accepted the praise. He'd been thankful for the opportunity to prove himself, and his uncle had given him the tools and confidence he'd needed.

If Matterson Consulting garnered more business from the Boeing Company, Jayson was certain that his uncle Matthew would hand the company reins over to him when he retired. That was what Jayson wanted, what he strived to accomplish, and this report went a long way toward making that desire a possibility.

As he entered his office, Jayson's cellphone rang. He reached inside his pocket and saw that it was Cooper.

"Hey," Jayson greeted, happy to connect with his best friend. "What's up?"

"Not much. Thinking about Christmas."

As far as Jayson was concerned, there wasn't much to think about. Christmas was like any other day to him. By choice, he ignored the holiday, seeing that it brought up nothing but unwelcome memories.

"You got plans for Christmas with that new girl of yours?" Cooper asked. He'd been on Jayson from the first about Merry, digging for information. For the most part, Jayson had been able to sidestep his questions.

Except one.

Like a dog after a bone, Cooper wanted to know about their meeting. The meeting that had never happened. Each time

Jayson put him off, his cousin had grown more suspicious.

"Merry and I haven't made plans yet," he said, which was true.

"In case you haven't noticed, Christmas is only a few days away."

"I know." Looking to divert Cooper's questions, he asked, "What about you and Maddy?"

"I'll be with her family. You met Merry's family yet?"

"Not yet. How are the wedding plans coming along?"

Cooper exhaled a long, slow sigh. "I have to tell you, man, I had no idea a wedding would take this much planning. Far as I'm concerned, we could stand barefoot on a beach and be done with it. Maddy's got a completely different idea. There are flowers and musicians, and a catered dinner at this posh resort. Her mother is involved with the plans now, and I swear there was less involved in the construction of the Great Wall of China."

Jayson couldn't squelch his laughter. "Next thing I know you'll be wanting me to wear a tux by the pool."

"I have no idea what Maddy and her mother are going to want. For now, I'm staying out of it. I'm on a need-to-know basis."

"Probably the best way to handle that."

"Now quit avoiding the subject. I want to know how it's going with your girl."

Jayson's smile slowly faded. "It's going great." And it was, except for that one blip. But they were communicating again, and that was what mattered to him.

"I want to hear what she's like in person."

Jayson sighed, which seemed to prompt more questions from his cousin.

"She was a disappointment, wasn't she?"

"No." Seeing that they'd never met face-to-face, he could say that in all honesty.

"Was she everything you expected?"

Jayson hesitated, considered lying, and then decided he needed to be honest. His shoulders sagged and he released a sigh. "I guess I might as well tell you. She didn't show."

His answer was followed by a heavy silence.

"She didn't show?" Cooper repeated.

"You heard me right." He bristled, irritated that his cousin could get him to confess what had happened.

"Why not?"

This was where it got tricky. "I'm not exactly sure. She said she knew me."

"So?"

"Well, it seems she'd already met me. I just have no idea when or where. Apparently, I didn't leave a good impression." Jayson had racked his brain to figure what could have happened. All he could think was that he'd had an especially bad day and overreacted to something, but if that was the case, he didn't remember it. "We set a time and place to meet. Merry took one look at me at our designated spot and had a change of heart, deciding it was best that we not get involved."

Cooper was outraged on his behalf. "What the—"

"I talked her into giving me another chance," Jayson said, cutting off his cousin before he went on a tangent.

"Hold on," Cooper said, his words coated with annoyance. "You talked to her?"

"Not talk talked. But online talked."

"Man, I have to tell you, I haven't met this girl, but I have serious doubts. You're a catch, and if she doesn't recognize that, then be done with her."

Cooper had always been his staunchest supporter.

"I briefly considered that," Jayson admitted. "I have to admit my ego took a direct hit, and like you, I thought, whatever. If that was what she wanted, then so be it, but as the days went by I found myself thinking about her more and more. Going online with her was and is the highlight of my day. I look forward to that time with her as much as I do my first cup of coffee in the morning. More so."

Cooper appeared to be weighing his words. "You like her that much?"

"I do."

"You don't think all this talk is an excuse on her part? She could be hiding something."

"I doubt it." This was something Jayson had considered himself. Of course, it was possible, but he didn't think it was true with Merry. "Everything I know about her tells me she's a straight shooter."

"I hope you're right," Cooper said in that thoughtful way of his. "You've always had good instincts, so if this girl is as special as you seem to think, then go for it."

Jayson grinned. "I appreciate the vote of confidence. The thing is, there's this other . . ." He hesitated, wondering if he should say anything about his unexpected attraction to Mary from data entry.

"Other what?" Cooper pressed.

Once again Jayson tried to avoid the subject. "I've been involved in putting together this report."

"Yeah, yeah, I know all about that. You've been working for weeks on that Boeing project."

"My hours have been crazy, and frankly there hasn't been time to date. Merry is busy at her job, too."

"Jayson, come on, man, give it up. What aren't you telling me?"

Cooper knew him far too well.

"Something about working all these hours. Spill, Jay."

"Okay, okay, there's this girl in the office that's been a big help to me and I sort of find her attractive." That was a gross understatement, but he didn't want to admit how attracted he was to her, even to himself.

"Then ask her out. It might bring Merry around if she knows she has competition."

The idea had started to take root long before Cooper's suggestion. It went without saying that this was problematic for several reasons. He didn't want to play one woman against the other. He'd seen far too much of this very thing from his parents and their various marriages. Lots of other reasons came to mind, too.

"I can't date her."

"Because she's an employee?" Cooper picked up on that right away.

"Well, that, too, although she's only a temp. But that isn't the only problem."

"Then what is?"

Jayson stared at the ceiling and exhaled slowly. "She's dating someone else."

"Have you two spent time together?"

"A little," he confessed.

"Is she interested in you?"

Jayson needed to mull this over before he answered, being as truthful with himself as he could be. "I think she is."

"Then make your move," Cooper advised. "If this other guy was important, she wouldn't be sending you vibes."

"Vibes? Mary's not sending me vibes."

"Wait. What did you say her name was?"

"Mary. M-a-r-y, not to be confused with M-e-r-r-y."

Cooper chuckled. "I am confused. You're attracted to two women, both of whom are named Mary, but spelled differently."

"Yup."

"How is it that you find more ways to

complicate your life than anyone else I know?"

Jayson had to agree and then chuckled. "Yes. But I'll never have a problem confusing their names, now, will I?"

"That you won't," Cooper agreed. "Listen, keep me updated on what happens. Guess I'll tell Maddy you'll be bringing a date to the wedding, and most likely her name will be Mary."

Jayson grinned. All he had to do now was figure out which Mary it would be.

CHAPTER ELEVEN

✳

Merry

Merry was just about to leave the office Friday night when she got word that Jayson Bright had asked to speak to her. He sent his assistant, Mrs. Bly, to fetch her. She was a middle-aged woman who was rumored to have been with Matterson Consulting since its infancy.

Merry was immediately suspicious that Jayson had somehow uncovered who she was—her real identity. He'd requested that she come directly to his office.

Perhaps she'd made a mistake with the data on Friday that had completely messed up the report. In which case he would be angry and he'd fire her on the spot. Would he do that? Especially now, when only a little more than a week remained in her contract?

"You in trouble with the boss again?" Lauren asked as soon as Mrs. Bly left.

Kylie shook her head at Merry. "Hey, think positive. Maybe he's giving you a bonus for staying late last Friday."

"I didn't do anything wrong. I swear." She hoped.

"Well, don't keep him waiting," Lauren said, shooing her away with both hands. "But keep us in the loop. If the company is handing out pink slips, I need to know about it."

With her heart bouncing up and down in her throat like it was on a pogo stick, Merry approached the executive area of the office.

Mrs. Bly had returned to her desk, and

when she noticed Merry, she said, "You can go right in. Mr. Bright is waiting."

Merry knocked once and then slowly opened the door to his office. Jayson sat at his desk, leaning back in his chair with his hands on the back of his head. He appeared to be deep in thought and didn't notice her for a few awkward moments.

When he did, he looked at her and blinked, as if finding her standing in the doorway to his office was completely unexpected.

"You asked to see me?" she reminded him. Her hands felt clammy and she gripped them in front of her, literally holding on to herself. She felt as if she was in junior high and had been called to the principal's office.

"Yes, yes." He gestured for her to come inside. "Close the door, if you would."

She did as he asked and remained standing, moving closer to his desk.

"Please sit down. You might be a few minutes."

She sank into the chair, sitting on the edge of the seat. The high-back chair was made of buttery soft leather and vastly unlike her own uncomfortable desk chair.

As if to make her even more nervous, Jayson continued to stare at her as though looking straight through her. She swallowed hard, convinced now that he'd managed to guess the truth.

Waiting for him to speak was torture. Merry did her best to be patiently composed, although her nails dug into the tender part of her palms, leaving deep indentations. Her heart continued to pound, but this time hard enough to play drums in a rock band. If Jayson was going to explode, then it was important that she remain calm and serene, no matter what.

"I imagine you're wondering why I asked to speak to you."

Because her mouth had gone dry, she nodded rather than respond verbally.

"Don't worry, this has nothing to do with your job."

That didn't reassure her. She glanced at her watch, wondering if she would make her bus.

Noticing that she looked at the time, he said, "This might take awhile. Will that be a problem for you?"

"No, but I'd like to know how long I'll be."

He cocked his brow and asked with a grin, "Another date?"

"No. If I'm going to miss the bus, then I'll need to make a phone call."

"You share an apartment with friends? Not that it's any of my business, of course." He was showing more curiosity about her now than he had in all the time she'd worked for the company. Merry couldn't help wondering what that meant, if anything. "Never mind. If you miss the bus, then I'll be happy to drive you home."

"There'll be other buses I can catch, don't worry. And no, I don't mind telling you. I live in a house."

"Rent being what it is, I suppose you have roommates," he commented. His eyes widened and he raised his hand. "Sorry, I did it again. None of my business."

Merry smiled, enjoying his discomfort. She liked that he wanted to know more about her and then realized she was competing with herself. It seemed silly to be jealous of the other woman when **she was the other woman.**

"Do you need me to stay late again? I can."

"No, no, the project is completed."

He didn't seem to be in a hurry to get to the point. His scrutiny made her uncomfortable. All he seemed to want to do was intently look at her, to study her every feature. He seemed hesitant, as if unsure of himself, which was nothing like the Jayson Bright she knew.

"Is something wrong with my appearance?" Merry asked, looking down at her outfit. She wore a green-and-blue jacket and a pencil skirt with knee-high boots. She couldn't imagine he would find fault with that.

"Your appearance?" he repeated, shaking his head. "No. Not at all. You look great. More than great. Lovely."

He was complimenting her. This was strange and it worried her. If she sat any closer to the edge of the chair she was sure to slip off and land on her butt, which would be terribly embarrassing.

"I wanted to personally thank you for everything you did to help me finish the Boeing report," he said. "Having you enter the last bit of information made a big difference."

"I was happy to help."

"I understand that, and it's appreciated. I realize we've had our share of differences in the past, but you haven't let that affect your work."

"Thank you." His praise embarrassed her. Little did he know how happy she was to spend that time with him. She'd seen more of the Jay she knew from her online chats with him than Jayson, her boss. He'd been grateful and considerate. A week or two ago she hadn't been able to see that side of him. That one evening showed her there was more to Jayson Bright than she'd realized.

"I understand you were hired short-term by an agency," Jayson continued, cutting into her thoughts.

"My contract was for a year." Even though she'd been with the company for nearly twelve months, he hadn't paid much attention to her until the last few weeks, when the deadline for the report was pressing.

"That long?" He arched his eyebrows

with the question, as though taken by surprise.

She did her best to hide a smile.

"At any rate, I wanted you to know if you're looking for a permanent position, I'd welcome you on staff."

This was unexpected, and for a moment she struggled to find words. For him to offer her a position was more than she'd ever considered. Her big fear coming into his office was that he wanted to fire her before her contract was completed. She'd never even suspected that he'd been considering giving her a permanent position. "I . . . I hardly know what to say. Thank you. That you would make such an offer means a great deal. It's tempting. This is a good company and the benefits are certainly appealing, but I've already registered for college classes." She'd been saving as much money as she could, in hopes of pursuing her goal to become a special education teacher.

"I didn't realize you were a college student." He frowned, as though wondering when she found the time to squeeze classes in with a forty- or fifty-hour work-week.

Merry felt she should explain. "I took the year off from school to save up enough to finish my last year. If all goes according to plan, I should have my teaching certificate by this time next year."

He nodded approvingly, as though he could see her in front of a classroom. "You'll be a good teacher, Mary. You have the patience and the temperament."

"I enjoy children, and it seemed a natural choice for me." She didn't mention her interest in special education, for fear he would make the connection between her and Patrick.

"I imagine you're eager to head home."

"I'm in no rush." She had plenty of time to catch the next bus; in fact, she had time to kill.

Jayson stood and escorted her to the door. "I'll see you at the Christmas party, right?"

"Actually, no."

"No?"

"I have plans that evening. Of course, you'll be there."

"Yes, it's more or less mandatory." Jayson walked to the door and opened it for her. She noticed that Mrs. Bly had already left for the evening, as had nearly all the staff. After all these weeks of mandatory overtime, it seemed everyone was eager to leave the office as quickly as possible.

"When is your last day?" Jayson asked. Seeing that she wouldn't be working between Christmas and New Year's, it was coming up quickly. "The twenty-third, the day of the Christmas party."

"It's coming right up, then?"

"Yes. It's been a good year."

He grinned, his gaze warm. "Yes, it has. It's been a very good year on several different levels. Have a good evening, Mary."

Merry returned to her desk, collected her coat and purse, and headed out of the building. Because she had nearly an hour to wait for the next bus, she decided to grab dinner. It was her turn to cook, and because she was going to be an hour late, she would bring the meal home rather than keep everyone waiting on their food.

The New York deli a few blocks over was said to have a great reputation. She could easily grab something to go and make it to the bus stop in plenty of time. Splurging on herself and her family would be a treat.

Walking to the deli, her mood was high following her conversation with Jayson. When she arrived at the deli, she could see that they did a robust business, if the long line of customers was any indication. Glancing at her watch, she decided she had the time to wait in line, and she started reading over the menu posted behind the counter. A familiar voice spoke from behind her.

Jayson Bright.

"We meet again," he said. "You come here often?"

"No, it's my first time. Lauren recommended it and I thought I'd give it a try. I've got time before the next bus." The line, however, didn't seem to be moving all that quickly. "I think I do anyway."

"It's a popular place."

"So I see. What about you? You come here often?"

He shrugged. "Often enough to be on a first-name basis."

The line moved forward one person. Merry kept her hands buried in her coat pockets.

"Listen," Jayson said. "Would you consider letting me take you to dinner? To thank you. No obligation, just dinner between friends."

The question hung in the air between them with the tension of a tightrope.

"If you're thinking it's against company policy to date an employee," he quickly added, "then you're right. But technically you're not an employee of the company, so I feel confident I'm not going against company rules. And it's not really a date anyway. Just friends, remember?"

Merry couldn't help it—she laughed out loud. "You really **are** a stickler for the rules, aren't you?"

"No, I simply wanted to assure you that you're under no obligation to accept. No harm, no foul."

"Then I'll gladly accept. I'll need to make a call first, though."

He grinned. "Then you're game?"

She nodded, her smile so big her mouth hurt. This was a night filled with surprises. She'd been afforded a different side of Jayson Bright, and now he was giving her another opportunity to know him on a completely different level. "Sure, why not? Dinner between friends."

"What's your favorite food?" he asked. "Steak? Italian? Greek? Mexican?"

Over the weeks, they'd had extensive conversations about their likes and dislikes. She knew Jayson was a meat-and-potatoes kind of man. "A steak dinner sounds wonderful."

His eyes revealed his pleasure in her choice. "You make your phone call and I'll see about reservations."

"Deal." Merry couldn't hide her joy. Wanting privacy, she said, "I'll meet you outside."

Jayson already had his phone out and had it pressed against his ear.

As soon as Merry was outside the deli, she called the house. Patrick answered. "Hey, Patrick, any chance you could take care of dinner tonight for you and Mom?" Their dad was on an overnight business trip to Yakima, in the center of the state.

"It's your turn to cook," he reminded her. Patrick was the one who made up the schedule.

"I know. This is special, though."

"What are you doing?" he asked suspiciously.

"I have a date," she told him. This whole craziness had started because Patrick and her mother didn't think she got out enough.

"A date?" her brother pried. "With who?"

Merry lowered her voice. "My boss."

She could feel her brother's disapproval radiate over the phone. "You shouldn't do that. Jay wouldn't like you dating someone else."

It would be too complicated to explain everything to her brother. "It's fine, Patrick. I promise you, Jay won't mind at all. Can you take care of you and Mom tonight?"

"Okay. I can make chili with chips. I like chili with chips."

Not her mother's favorite meal, but she would eat it gladly when Patrick told her why Merry wouldn't be home for dinner that evening. "Okay. Thanks."

Merry ended the call at about the same time she saw Jayson approach. "I couldn't get a reservation until seven. I hope you don't mind waiting."

Glancing at the time on her phone, she saw that they had sixty minutes to spare. A later dinner gave her even more time to spend with Jayson, allowing her to get to know him better without him suspecting she was Merry.

Dangerous game or not, she couldn't be more pleased or excited.

CHAPTER TWELVE

✳

Jayson

"The restaurant is only a few blocks away," Jayson mentioned. "I hope you don't mind walking." The weather was relatively clear, although chilly. He enjoyed the cold, clear weather. His favorite time of year was winter, when the sky was blue and the cold air was crisp. He'd grab them a cab if Mary deemed it necessary, but he'd prefer the walk.

"Yes, please. It would be fun to see all the Christmas displays. I haven't had much of a chance to do that yet this year."

"You mean because of all the overtime?" he said, half jokingly. He felt bad about that, but there'd been no other option if he intended to get that report in on time.

"That, and for other reasons, too. I love the lights, the street vendors selling their wares, and there's usually a few caroling groups around Pacific Place. Would you mind?"

How could he refuse in the face of such enthusiasm? He walked to and from the office every day and hadn't noticed a single thing Mary had mentioned. "I think we could manage that and still make it to the restaurant in time."

"Great." She rubbed her hands together eagerly.

They walked away from the deli, and Jayson placed his hand at the small of her back, guiding her. She glanced his way and smiled. Such a simple gesture from her, and yet it touched him and he found himself smiling back. Jayson wasn't one who smiled freely. It felt strange and he realized he hadn't done nearly enough of that in the last few weeks. The relief he felt getting that report into Boeing was a huge weight off his shoulders.

As they crossed the street, Jayson's thoughts drifted to Merry. They'd made no official plans to chat that evening, though they usually connected every night, with few exceptions, at around eight-thirty, nine at the latest. It would do him good to miss a night, to keep her guessing. He didn't owe her an explanation. As much as he wanted to believe what they shared was real, his cousin's doubts had left him questioning his judgment. He'd never been one ruled by emotion. He wanted to believe Merry was everything she'd said, and that left him vulnerable in ways that made him uncomfortable. Skipping a night might be exactly what was needed for her to agree to meet.

Being it was the holidays, Jayson found the streets crowded with last-minute Christmas shoppers. Someone bumped into Mary and she stumbled forward a step. Jayson steadied her and then wrapped her arm around his elbow, surprised by how much he enjoyed the sense of being linked with her. He placed his hand over hers, sorry he wore gloves, as he'd enjoy the feel of her hand in his.

"There doesn't seem to be much of that goodwill toward mankind left these days," he commented.

"Oh, but there is," she insisted, looking up at him. "You just have to look for it. I promise you it's there." She pointed toward the woman who stood in front of Nordstrom, ringing a bell to remind those rushing about on the street of those less fortunate. "There's a good example."

She was right. Another woman stood on the corner, handing out notices for a church that was holding a free dinner for anyone who cared to attend. Mary took the flyer and read it aloud to him. "See?" she asked.

"Okay, you win. All I need to do is open my eyes."

"Oh look," Mary cried, hurrying their steps as she steered them toward a street vendor.

"What's this?" Jayson asked. The man at the cart had a pot going and people had lined up, waiting their turn.

"Roasted chestnuts," Mary said excitedly. "Let's get some."

"This is a real thing? Roasted chestnuts sound like something out of a Dickens novel."

"It does, and yes, it's a real thing."

"I'm happy to buy you some, but they don't sound all that appetizing to me."

"Give it a chance. They actually taste quite good."

Jayson was game to give them a try. He'd passed this vendor any number of times on his walk to and from the office but hadn't bothered to investigate.

They joined the queue and Mary gave him a brief rundown on what to expect, flavor-wise. Jayson didn't pay much attention to what she said; all he seemed capable of hearing was the sweet joy that radiated from her. It touched him in a way he found difficult to ignore. The more time he spent with Mary, the less his thoughts drifted to Merry. He felt drawn to her, almost as if he'd known her far longer and better than their limited contact accounted for.

When it was their turn, Jayson bought the chestnuts and had his first sample. He bit into the warm crunch and raised his brows, noticing that he had Mary's attention. She was right, they weren't half bad.

"Well," she asked, studying him. "What do you think?"

He shrugged. "Like you said, they're tasty."

"For me, it's more the novelty of it," Mary told him. She removed her glove and dipped two fingers into the bag to help herself to a second one. "Thank you for this."

He brushed off her appreciation, slightly embarrassed by her gratitude for such a small thing. They continued their walk with Jayson holding the bag of warm chestnuts, munching as they headed down the street toward the restaurant.

As they neared the corner, a group of singers dressed in Victorian garb approached. The women wore long wool coats with fur collars and had their hands inside matching fur muffs. The men were dressed in dark wool coats with top hats. Their voices blended in perfect harmony as they strolled along singing, "God Rest Ye Merry Gentlemen."

Jayson steered Mary back as the singers moved past. He noticed a dreamy look come over her, as if their music was equal to that of the angels.

"Aren't they wonderful?" she asked, smiling, eyes clean and bright with happiness.

For the first few moments, he was mesmerized by her smile. Thankfully, the question was rhetorical and didn't require an answer. Experiencing the joy of the season with her brought a new appreciation of the holidays. Christmas was just another day to him. He'd never paid that much attention to many aspects of the holiday season. But then, he acknowledged he never really had celebrated it. Oh, there'd been gifts. His fractured family had always seen to giving him material goods. But it was the important things like time, attention, love, and any kind of nurturing that had been sadly absent. It was as if his parents didn't know what to do with a child. Their gifts meant nothing to him. He routinely gave them away. He viewed their gifts as attempts to assuage their guilt for abandoning him. His refusal to accept their presents was his way of letting them know he couldn't be bought.

It started to snow—light flakes that drifted down from the heavens like small feathers released from angel pillows. Mary was beside herself with joy, tilting her head toward the sky and letting the flakes fall on her face.

"I've always loved catching snow on my eyelashes."

"What?"

"The song 'My Favorite Things' from **The Sound of Music.** Surely you remember that?"

He had seen the movie, but that had been years and years ago. "Sure," he said, "I remember it."

"I'd so hoped it would snow. This is perfect, just perfect." She all but danced down the sidewalk, dragging him along with her.

He stared at her in disbelief. The woman was nuts. Snow complicated everything, and even a small accumulation had the potential to cripple the city, causing all kinds of problems. Seattle didn't deal well with snow. A few inches were enough to paralyze the city.

"I hope it doesn't stick," he muttered. He was willing to admit he enjoyed her enthusiasm. He was more practical, though.

"You're joking." Mary looked at him like he'd suddenly sprouted horns. "It's almost Christmas," she reminded him. "Who doesn't long for a white Christmas? This is perfect." She threw out her arms and twirled around like a child on the playground.

Jayson grinned, finding her enthusiasm infectious. "Okay, okay, you're right. Snow is . . . beautiful and the timing is perfect, especially for kids."

"Christmas is the most wonderful time of the year."

"For some," he whispered, thinking she wouldn't hear.

She did.

"It's more than a season," she said, wrapping her arm around his elbow and leaning her head against his shoulder.

Her familiarity surprised him. With anyone else he would have been taken aback, but for reasons he had yet to explore, he felt completely at ease with Mary. He found nothing pretentious about her. She was real and genuine, unlike many of the women he'd dated in the past. Not that this was a date . . .

"Christmas is a condition of the heart," she continued, and as she spoke she planted a hand over her chest. "It's being open and sincere, generous and kind to those with less, or showing our love to those we cherish." She stopped talking abruptly and glanced at him with a guilty look. "Sorry, I didn't mean to get on a soap box."

He smiled down at her, enjoying her more than he ever expected he would. As they walked toward the restaurant, Mary made multiple stops to gaze into the shop windows, pointing out little things he didn't notice in the displays, or along their walk, like the shining star in the distance atop Macy's department store.

"You know if it'd been three wise **women** searching for the newborn babe, they would have asked for directions much sooner, found the stable, swept it out, and had a meal waiting by the time Mary and Joseph arrived."

Jayson chuckled and shook his head. "No comment."

They saw children behind a display window of Santa's Workshop, waiting in line to visit Santa. Parents stood with them as the children squirmed. Jayson couldn't imagine the nightmare of standing in line with a bunch of fussy kids. Mary, however, had exactly the opposite reaction.

"Aren't the children adorable?"

He looked again, and all he saw were little ones clinging to their parents. A few were asleep on their father's shoulders and others were holding on to a mother's leg, terrified of meeting the oddly dressed man with a white beard.

"I feel sorry for them."

"Sorry?" The look she gave him suggested he was a space alien.

"Look at those parents," he commented. "They're exhausted, the kids are fussy, and Santa looks like he's completely worn out."

"That's what you see?" she asked, sounding shocked.

"You mean you don't?"

"No!" She stopped in front of the window. "I see that little girl in the ballerina-style dress entertaining her little brother and telling him all about Santa and those two mothers chatting happily, sharing experiences and information. As for Santa, he's the best. When I was small, my mother brought me to have my photo taken with Santa. I was so excited I could barely stand still. She still has the photo of me on his lap. I'm looking up at him adoringly. I savored the candy cane I got from him, and licked on it for three days."

Jayson paused, trying to see it through Mary's eyes, and realized she was right. Yes, there were a couple disgruntled and cranky children. The majority, however, were excited and happy, patiently waiting their turn.

When they reached the restaurant, their timing was perfect and they were seated immediately. They were given an upholstered booth with poinsettias displayed along the wall behind them.

Mary glanced around at the lushly decorated interior with the gold wall sconces and original artwork.

"Oh my goodness," she whispered, looking over the top of the menu, her eyes widening more by the moment. "I just saw the mayor of Seattle."

Jayson grinned. "It's one of the better steakhouses in town."

Her eyes grew even bigger when she reviewed the menu. He speculated she was looking at the prices.

She pressed the glossy menu to her chest and elbowed him before she whispered, "The cost of one steak here would feed a family for a week."

Jayson was busy studying the list of steaks. "Order whatever you'd like."

"I can't let you spend this kind of money on me," she said, keeping her voice low, as if afraid someone might overhear.

Jayson ignored her protest.

When the server approached, Jayson ordered a bottle of Malbec, one of his favorites. He talked her into sampling a glass.

The meal was everything he knew it would be. They carried on a conversation over the wine, and as he had earlier, Jayson found himself enjoying her company more and more. He casually mentioned Merry, explaining she was someone he'd met online but had yet to meet personally. Mary asked a few questions about that relationship. He felt comfortable enough to ask her advice about meeting a stranger online, and she admitted to doing it herself recently.

As they chatted, he sensed his feelings drifting away from Merry and toward Mary. He was interested in learning what he could about her. She had a close forever friend, who she hadn't seen in several months, and Mary missed her terribly. She told him about Lauren and Kylie, the two women she worked with in data entry. He avoided asking her about the man she was dating. If the two were serious, then it was doubtful she would have agreed to dine with him.

When they'd finished eating dinner, Mary leaned back against the cushioned booth and placed her hands on her stomach. "Wow, that was amazing," she said, sighing the words.

The dinner was excellent, he'd agree, but the company was more so.

Jayson couldn't remember a meal he'd enjoyed more. The steak was cooked to perfection, and watching Mary eat was a delight. She savored every bite and cleaned her plate. He enjoyed the fact that she enjoyed her food and didn't stress over every calorie.

When it came time to order dessert, she declared, "I couldn't stuff down another bite."

"Would you like to take one home for later?" he asked.

"I can do that?"

From her reaction, one would think he'd offered her shares in a gold mine. "Of course."

She couldn't seem to decide between the cheesecake and the chocolate cake.

"She'll take both," Jayson instructed the waiter.

A few minutes later, the waiter delivered a take-out bag containing the two desserts, along with the bill.

Leaving the restaurant, Mary checked her watch. "I have ten minutes to the next bus."

"No, you don't," he stated calmly.

"But I do. The bus comes fifteen minutes past the hour, every hour."

"Mary, I am not letting you ride the bus home. I'm driving you."

Her eyes got as big as dinner plates. "You're willing to face the Seattle traffic on a Friday night?" she asked, as if he needed to seriously reconsider.

"I insist on driving you home, so your answer is yes."

"But . . ."

"No arguments." He took her hand and led her to the high-rise where he kept his vehicle. The homeless man who'd taken to sleeping on the corner remained there, sitting over the grate. He glanced up at them.

To Jayson's amazement, Mary stopped walking, pulled her hand free of Jayson's, and started a conversation with the man. Thankfully, the conversation was a short one. Then, before he could stop her, Mary removed the chocolate cake from the bag and handed it to him, along with the plastic spoon.

"Merry Christmas," she told the man, and then rejoined Jayson.

"You're only encouraging him," he muttered once they were out of earshot.

"Maybe," she agreed, "but my guess is

he's never had any dessert that will taste nearly as good as that chocolate cake."

And likely one that hadn't cost that much, either. Jayson didn't begrudge the man the ultra-rich dessert. He was in for a treat.

The doorman greeted Jayson and looked mildly surprised to find him with a guest. Jayson led Mary into the garage and to his assigned parking spot.

After opening the car door for her, she stared at all the lights and features in the car. After giving him her home address, he entered it into his navigational system and exited the garage.

They shared a companionable silence on the ride home. He enjoyed the fact that Mary didn't feel the need to fill the quiet and that she was content to sit in the heavy flow of commuters and listen to the music playing on the radio. Rarely had he been more aware of a woman at his side.

Mary was completely unpretentious and unlike any woman he'd ever known. Jayson was willing to admit that driving her home had been an excuse to spend more time with her. Already he was thinking of excuses so he could see her again.

He parked in front of her house. One look at the three-story Victorian told Jayson that this was more than a house. It was a home. Brightly lit wreaths with big red bows hung from nearly every window. The porch was surrounded by cheerful lights.

Mary interrupted his thoughts, and he took his eyes off her home.

"I had the most wonderful evening," she was saying. "Thank you for everything."

"I did, too," he returned, and it was no exaggeration. Her dimple deepened as she looked at him. He couldn't take his eyes off it. He found her one dimple simply adorable.

He **should** climb out of the car and walk her to the door, he thought, but he couldn't make himself move. Mary glanced his way and it looked for a moment as if she had something on her mind. All he could do was hope it was the same thing that was on his.

Leaning forward, he pressed his mouth to hers. The kiss was gentle, more a grazing of their lips. A testing. Her mouth was moist and soft, so incredibly soft. Right away he knew it wasn't near enough to satisfy him and he wanted more. Needed more. Tucking his hand along the base of her neck, he brought her closer, deepening the exchange. To his delight, she leaned in to him, opening herself to him and sighing with pleasure. On second thought, he might have been the one who breathed out his own need, his own pleasure.

As sensation filled him, Jayson felt as

though a weight had been lifted from him, freeing him from the burdens of his youth. A heady rightness that was physical as well as emotional crept over him. He'd been kissing girls since he was thirteen, but he'd never felt anything even close to what he did with Mary. He slowly released her and sat back, wondering what this might mean.

Following the kiss, all that either of them was able to do was stare at each other in total amazement at what had just happened. Mary smiled and then he did, too, unsure if she felt anything even close to what he had.

She must have. How could she not?

He braced his forehead against hers and resisted the urge to kiss her again, afraid that if he did, he wouldn't be able to stop.

"I should go inside," she whispered, and then cleared her throat as if she found it difficult to get the words out.

"I'll see you Monday."

"Okay. It's my last day in the office."

"I know." To his way of thinking, that was good news. She wouldn't be working for him, which meant no one from the office need know they were seeing each other. He assumed they would continue dating. He couldn't imagine not seeing Mary again.

He walked her to the door and was strongly tempted to kiss her again but restrained himself. With her hand on the door handle, she hesitated. "Thank you again for everything."

"I appreciated the advice about online dating," he said, reminding her of their earlier discussion at the restaurant.

"Sure. Anytime."

"Listen," he said, stopping her by placing his hand on her forearm. All at once it became important to make sure this was only the beginning and not the end.

"Would you like to go out again . . . sometime? When it's convenient for us both? I know you're seeing someone else, so if I'm stepping on anyone's toes, I apologize." If she was serious about the other man, then she'd let him know.

"I'd like that," she said without hesitation, her face alive with a smile, as though she wanted this as much as he did.

"And this guy you're seeing that you met online . . . ?" He left the question hanging, eager to hear her response.

"Aren't you involved with someone online as well?" she asked without answering him.

Merry.

Jayson wanted to slap his forehead, aghast that she had completely slipped his mind. "Yes, of course. I need to resolve that."

She smiled and then kissed his cheek. "I've got a relationship to resolve myself."

He waited for her to open the door and step inside before he returned to his car and headed back into the city.

Once back at his condo, Jayson decided to log on to his computer to see if Merry had left him a message.

He discovered she hadn't, but Patrick had.

Jayson, Merry isn't home from work yet. She won't be here when you want to talk to her. I thought you should know.

Dad got a jigsaw puzzle and we'll put that together Christmas Day. We do that every Christmas. It's fun, but I'm not good at finding the pieces. Merry helps me. Please don't be mad at Merry. And don't tell her I sent you a message, okay?

So while he was out on a date, Merry was working overtime. He felt a pang of guilt, not that he should. The guilt had to do with the fact that she had completely slipped his mind.

He grinned as he leaned back in his chair and stared at the computer screen. Like Cooper had said, only Jayson could become involved with two women with the same name. But Jayson was determined not to complicate his life. He had a decision to make and had a strong feeling about which way he leaned.

CHAPTER THIRTEEN

Merry

Merry woke Saturday morning with the most delicious feelings. Her evening with Jayson had been above and beyond anything she could have expected.

His kisses lingered in her mind, warming her.

She had no idea she could feel so much in a simple kiss. Thinking about it made her want to wrap her arms around herself and hold on to the memory. Their time together had been wonderful in every way. She loved the walk to the restaurant, sharing the bag of roasted chestnuts, listening to the wandering Victorian singers, glancing in the display windows and looking over the Christmas decorations. Merry couldn't remember a time she'd enjoyed more, and it had nothing to do with the fancy dinner. It was him, all him.

While they were parked outside the house, she was tempted to tell him she was the Merry he'd met online. But then he'd kissed her and that was the end of that.

She really needed to get up and help her mother, but before she could convince herself to leave the luxury of her bed . . .

"Merry?" Her brother called from the other side of her bedroom door.

No time to dwell on Jayson any longer. "Yes, Patrick?"

"Can I come in?"

"Sure." She sat up in bed and drew the covers up tighter around her torso to avoid the chill.

Her brother cracked open the door and peeked inside. His eyes avoided hers, which was a sure sign he'd done something he thought would displease her.

"Patrick?"

"It's Saturday."

"I know." He kept his gaze down on the floor.

"Is there something you want to tell me?"

Adamantly shaking his head, Patrick looked away, but not before she saw his eyes widen, as if he feared she'd been able to read his mind.

"Then why won't you look at me?"

He shuffled his feet. "Because if I look at you then you'll know."

"Know what?"

His shoulders lifted with a huge sigh. "Okay, I'll tell you. Last night when you went out with the mean boss . . ."

"He isn't mean . . . I just didn't know him."

Not to be dissuaded, her brother continued. "Anyway, while you were out I logged on to Mix & Mingle and left a message for Jay."

This should be interesting. "Did you tell him I was on a date with another man?" she asked.

His eyes shot open and became as round as golf balls. "No, I wouldn't do that. It would hurt his feelings."

That was her brother, hyper-aware of doing anything unkind.

"I told him you weren't home from work yet and not to be upset with you," he said, and then quickly added, "but I didn't say **why** he should be upset. It was okay to say that, right?"

"It's fine."

"Oh, and I told him about Dad buying the jigsaw puzzle to work on Christmas Day and that I need help finding the pieces and that you help me put them in place so I don't feel bad. I might not have said all that exactly, but that was what I was thinking." He chanced a look her way, keeping his head lowered. "You're not mad, are you?"

"Of course not. Who could be mad at you?"

"Sophie is. She wanted me to kiss her at the Christmas dance and I didn't want to because people were looking and she got mad."

"Is she still upset with you?"

He shook his head and then grinned. "I kissed her later in the dark."

Mentioning his kiss with Sophie reminded Merry of kissing Jayson, and she expelled a sigh.

"Hey, would you like to bake cookies this morning?" she asked, knowing baking was one of Patrick's favorite activities.

His face lit up with a huge smile. "Can we make the ones where you put your thumb in the cookie?"

"Sure, thumbprint cookies it is."

Saturday passed in a blur. After baking cookies with her brother, they delivered baked goods to the neighbors who had been helpful with Patrick and her mother. It was a small thing to do and showed their gratitude.

Later, Merry did the grocery shopping at a strip mall for the week. As she pushed the shopping cart toward the family car, she passed the window of a dress shop. Uncertain what caught her attention, she glanced at the outfit in the display. The dress was made of red silk, hitting about mid-thigh, with full length sleeves and a touch of lace at the fingertips. It was simple, chic, and spelled the holidays.

Mesmerized, Merry nearly stumbled before she could stop herself. For one crazed moment, she saw herself in that dress, walking toward Jayson when she revealed her identity. Merry would casually stroll toward him, the silk dress moving seductively against her body.

Jayson would be eagerly waiting to meet her. It would happen at the company Christmas party scheduled for Monday evening. There'd be music and champagne and magic in the air. Their eyes would meet and Jayson would be unable to look away from her. As she approached, his gaze would flare with appreciation, and he would be blinded by surprise that he had known her all along but hadn't realized the online woman was the very one he'd held and kissed. Then, unable to resist, he would hurry to meet her halfway. Naturally, he'd gently take her in his arms, and like the scene from one of her favorite romantic movies, **You've Got Mail**, he'd whisper in her ear, "I'd hoped it was you."

Well, she could dream, couldn't she?

It was silly, unrealistic, and about as far-fetched as Santa scooting down the chimney to deliver gifts. Nevertheless, the fantasy lingered in her mind.

Still, the lure of that dress was strong. Before she could give in to the temptation to go in and try it on, she pushed the shopping cart into the parking lot and unloaded the groceries and headed home.

Saturday evening Merry logged on at eight-thirty, their normal time. Sure enough, Jay was waiting for her.

Hey, she wrote.

Hey! Missed talking to you last night. Don't tell me that boss you're always complaining about made you stay late again.

Didn't realize I complained that much about my boss.

All the time, but you haven't so much lately.

Yes, well, I've had a change of heart about him.

Oh?

He's not half bad. I've come to like him quite a bit, actually.

I've always pictured him as old and cranky. He's not?

Nope. Young, your age, and good-looking, too.

There was a pause before Jay responded.

Are you trying to make me jealous?

Not really. I think we all need to have a more generous attitude toward others, especially this time of year.

Ah, Christmas. What is it with women and Christmas?

She read the message twice, unsure of his tone. It almost seemed that he was dismissing her Christmas spirit. Merry chose not to look at it that way.

I do love Christmas.

Speaking of which, I'm anxious for us to meet.

Oh?

It's time.

Yes, I suppose it is.

Past time. I don't want to be put off again.

I understand.

Good.

Tell me when and where and I'll be there.

His answer showed up almost immediately. The company where I work is in the downtown area, which I assume is relatively close for you. We have a Christmas party scheduled Monday evening. You should come.

He listed the address and told her the time.

I'll be there.

I'll look forward to meeting you at last.

Me, too.

They chatted for a bit longer until Patrick told her he needed the computer. He wanted to email Sophie. She explained to Jayson that the family had only the one computer. Merry would like nothing better than to get her brother his own; with only one laptop in the house, they were all forced to share. Merry so often controlled it in the evenings now that she felt obligated to get off when asked.

Sunday morning, the family was up early for church. Because this was the last Sunday before Christmas, the choir was going to perform the cantata. Patrick was excited, and his enthusiasm rubbed off on Merry.

She'd spent a restless night, planning how best to reveal herself to Jayson the following evening at the company Christmas party. She wanted it to be a welcome surprise and not one that would upset or embarrass him. As she pondered what was best, regrets crowded her mind. Not revealing herself to Jayson had gone on far longer than she'd ever intended. Everything hinged now on Jayson's reaction to her true identity.

She pictured him holding out his arms,

smiling at her. Then he'd tell her that he'd guessed it was her from the very beginning.

That was the best scenario and the one least likely.

Her mind reviewed another. In this one, his eyes were cold, his mouth pinched, all the while glaring at her and accusing her of playing him for a fool.

Always the optimist, Merry went for option number one. Not that she was completely convinced once he learned the truth he would be pleased. Delighted, even. Well, a girl could hope.

Following church, Merry had lunch with her family when the house phone rang.

Her mother answered. "Yes, hold on a minute, she's here," she said and handed the cordless receiver to Merry.

"Who is it?" she mouthed.

Robin shrugged but had a gleam in her eye. "**He** didn't say."

He? Now Merry was all the more curious. "Hello," she said tentatively.

"Hey."

Her heart leaped into her throat. It was Jayson. "Hi," she whispered, feeling giddy inside, a bit like she did in junior high when Mason Dunlap, a boy she'd liked, had phoned her.

"I hope you don't mind. I asked HR for your phone number earlier in case I needed any more help over the weekend. And I wanted you to know I've arranged to meet Merry."

"Merry?"

"Yes, the online woman I mentioned."

"Oh." Her heart started a drumroll beat, as if playing out taps before a firing squad.

"You were right to suggest we each resolve our other relationships," he said. "I gave her a time and place to meet."

"Didn't you mention at dinner that she'd left you hanging once? Rather rude of her, if you don't mind my saying so. Do you think she'll show this time?" she asked, her heart in her throat. She could almost feel her pulse hammering away on the side of her neck.

"I can't say."

"I bet she will." Merry did her best to hide her nervousness.

"It's her decision. If she doesn't, then I guess I'll know that it wasn't ever meant to be."

"From what you said Friday evening, you enjoyed your online chats and getting to know her."

"True," he agreed, albeit reluctantly, and then abruptly changed the subject. "I was calling to see how things are going with you."

In other words, he was asking if she'd followed through. "I . . . I haven't had a chance yet . . . you know. It's only been a couple days and . . ." She didn't know what more to say.

What she needed to do was tell Jayson, right then and there, that Mary was Merry, but it seemed wrong to blurt it out over the phone.

"I understand."

She was convinced she heard disappointment in his voice.

"Have you had a good weekend so far?"

"I have. You?"

He sighed softly. "I enjoyed getting to know you, Mary, and wish you the very best."

Lowering her voice, she whispered, "I enjoyed our time together, too."

Merry started to fill him in on her weekend activities when the phone beeped with an incoming call. "I should probably get that," she said, reluctant to let him go.

Beep.

"Are you sure you won't reconsider coming to the Christmas party Monday night?" he asked in a rush.

"No, sorry." She would be coming to the party, but as Merry, the woman he'd met online, not Mary, the temp.

"I'll see you at the office on Monday, then."

Beep.

"Good-bye, Jayson."

"Till Monday."

He disconnected, and Merry answered the call, which was from a friend of her mother's. Merry delivered the phone to her mother and then returned to the kitchen for dinner preparations.

As she worked, her mind sped ahead to the Christmas party. All she could do was hope for the best.

CHAPTER FOURTEEN

Jayson

For a good part of Monday, Jayson was on edge, anticipating meeting Merry, especially considering his growing attraction to Mary. This was technically her last day in the office. When he walked past the data-entry area earlier that morning, he noticed that her coworkers had brought in a small cake to celebrate the end of her contract.

Over dinner on Friday they'd talked about her future and her goals, and he'd mentioned a few of his own, surprised with the ease he felt discussing his life with her. She hadn't made a big deal out of it, but it was understood that money was tight with her family. When she spoke of her family it was with genuine love and affection. They were everything to her. Jayson had never felt that love or acceptance. She would create that same environment for her own husband and children one day. The man who married her would be fortunate.

From Mary, his thoughts automatically drifted to Merry. He was anxious to meet her in person. If she didn't show, he would delete his name from Mix & Mingle and scratch off the entire experiment as a learning experience.

He liked Merry. Genuinely liked her.

The thing was, he liked Mary, too. Ever since Friday, he hadn't been able to stop thinking about her.

He felt conflicted between the two women. His memories of all the nights he'd chatted online with Merry proved that she was more than a passing fancy. He'd spent more time getting to know her than any other woman he'd ever dated.

Dated.

That was the crazy part. They'd **never** dated. Never met. And yet he felt like he knew her.

Then there was Mary, whose eyes always snapped at him with irritation. Well, almost always. Things had changed between them. He barely knew her, and yet his feelings were strong. He was comfortable with her, at ease with no need to be anyone other than himself.

Either way, this was the day Jayson was convinced he would get clarity. In situations like this, the one person he felt comfortable talking to was his cousin.

He reached for his phone and punched the button that would connect him with Cooper.

"Merry Christmas," his cousin greeted.

"Back atcha," Jayson said, leaning back in his chair, relaxing.

"I bet I know why you're calling. You've finally met your dream girl."

"No."

"No you haven't met, or no that's not the reason you're phoning."

"Both, actually."

Cooper seemed to find his answer amusing. "What's going on?"

"I'm scheduled to meet Merry tonight," Jayson started off explaining. He wasn't sure what he expected Cooper to say. He'd never been one to openly share confidences, not the way his cousin did. Most everything that went on in his life was held close to his chest. Now there were two women, and he was confused and uncertain about what to do and how to handle these rare emotions. His focus had always been on his career and not on the nuances of women.

"It's about time," Cooper said. "You think she'll show?"

Who knew? Jayson pinched the bridge of his nose. "Don't know, and the truth is I'm of two minds."

His cousin took a moment to ponder his words. "What do you mean by that?"

Jayson wasn't sure he welcomed his cousin's counsel, but he trusted Cooper. He'd always had his back, and vice versa. It was how they'd managed to survive boarding school.

"I had a dinner date Friday night," Jayson admitted.

"The one you mentioned earlier? The other Mary?"

"Yeah." The image of Mary smiling up at him, reveling in the falling snow, trying to catch snowflakes on her eyelashes, brought a smile to his face. Every time he thought of their evening together, a warm, mushy, foreign sensation came over him.

He'd enjoyed every minute with her, and selfishly, he wanted more. Lots more.

"What is it about her that attracts you—well, other than her name?"

"Funny," Jayson muttered. "First off, she's bright and funny, and she's about as real as they come. Her work is impeccable, she's dedicated and hardworking and . . ."

"Hey, I'm not looking to hire her. What does she look like?"

"Cooper, there's more to a woman than looks." He might have sounded righteous, but he wasn't backing down. This was the lesson he'd learned with his online match. He didn't have a clue what Merry looked like physically. And to him it no longer mattered. It might have at one time, but he'd come to know her as a person. That was what had attracted him, kept his attention, kept him coming back to talk to her night after night. He'd enjoyed the opportunity to lower his guard and be himself behind the anonymity of the keyboard. Merry had absolutely no idea he would one day inherit a company, what he looked like, or how much money he had, which was an impressive amount, actually.

"I know, brother, I get that, but if she's beautiful, it can't hurt."

"What attracted you to Maddy?" Jayson asked. He remembered her as having frizzy, unmanageable auburn hair, braces, and thick glasses. Not exactly the classic beauty.

"Well, she's changed since we were in school together. A lot. The braces are long gone and so are the eyeglasses. She's beautiful," he said and laughed. "She's still got that crazy hair, sticking out in every which direction. It would be easier to tame a rattlesnake. But that crazy red hair is part of Maddy, and she's the one I love. She's the one I choose to spend the rest of my life with and I mean that with every fiber of my being. I'm not making the same mistake my parents made. This woman is it for me, man. One woman for the rest of my life."

Jayson pictured two or three children in his cousin's future with big, bright smiles and frizzy red hair. The image made him smile so big, his mouth ached.

"I get it," Jayson said, and he did. He realized he felt the same. Over the years, he hadn't given a lot of thought to marriage and a family. He'd seen the effects of divorce and wasn't willing to risk his heart. It surprised him that Cooper was willing to take the leap and trust the future. He loved Maddy enough to give it his all. That impressed Jayson more than he was willing to admit. It set him to thinking that a wife and family might be possible for him, too.

"Okay, tell me more about this other Mary."

"She's about five-five, maybe five-six,

slender. Brown hair and eyes, and she has the cutest dimple on one side of her mouth. Only one. It shows itself when she smiles and sometimes when she's irritated. I swear I can't take my eyes off her . . . I mean . . . the dimple."

"The dimple," Cooper repeated. "Listen, Jay, it sounds like you're hooked on this girl from the office."

"I am." He wasn't going to lie. Ever since they'd kissed, he had trouble remembering Merry, and then he'd go online and get involved in a conversation with Merry and be sucked into all those feelings. It reminded him of the dinghy he and his cousin would ride on the Puget Sound, when it became choppy. The swells would carry them up and down and up and down.

His heart wanted Mary.

And then it wanted Merry.

"So, tonight's the big night. Where are you meeting the online Merry?"

"Company Christmas party."

"You think that's a good idea? How's she going to know who you are with all those people floating around? And won't the other Mary be there as well?"

"You've forgotten that she's seen me before, Cooper, remember? And, no, the other Mary won't be there, which is a good thing. She said she had other plans."

"I'll be curious to see what happens and what you decide."

"Decide?"

"Yes, between Merry and Mary. You'll keep me updated, right?"

"Sure." He was grateful for Cooper helping him sort things out.

They ended the conversation. When Jayson looked at the clock, he was surprised to find it was time to head over to the Christmas party. The company had rented hotel space and the event planners had handled all the details, including decorations, music, food, and everything else. It was meant to be an elaborate affair. His uncle went all out with this party. This was the last full day of work before two paid holidays, Christmas Eve and Christmas Day, so everyone would be coming to the party directly from work in their business attire.

When Jayson walked into the Four Seasons, the room was filled with employees and their significant others.

He was greeted by a server with a tray of filled champagne glasses. He took one, sipped it, and smiled. Although it was a medium-priced label, the champagne wasn't bad. He'd looked over the food and wine budget and knew exactly the brand of sparkly that had been ordered.

Servers circulated the crowd with trays of appetizers. He was offered a variety of tasty hors d'oeuvres, all of which he refused. He wasn't in the mood for food. Wanting to get his official duties out of the way first, he greeted staff and made polite conversation with the executives and other colleagues. Once he was done making the rounds, he parked himself in the corner of the room and sipped his champagne.

He recognized most every employee but was unfamiliar with all their names. His gaze wandered over the room, seeking an unfamiliar face.

"Merry Christmas."

Mary joined him in his corner space, her eyes warm and her smile wide.

He frowned, distinctly remembering that she'd said she would be unable to attend the company Christmas party.

Her dimple was on full display, and he had a hard time looking away. "Merry Christmas," he returned. "I thought you couldn't make the party."

"I had a change in plans."

"That's great. I hope you enjoy yourself. Did you get a glass of champagne?" It took him a moment to realize he needed to pay more attention to the crowd in order not to miss identifying Merry.

"Not yet. By the way, I brought you a small gift."

Jayson took his gaze away from the crowd and turned to look at Mary. "Oh?"

"I baked you cookies. I stopped by the office and left them with Mrs. Bly. You'd already left for the party. I wanted you to know so you could bring them home."

"That wasn't necessary, but thanks."

"I told you I would, you know."

Jayson didn't remember that, but apparently, she had. He must not have been paying attention. He wouldn't make that same mistake now. He had an eagle eye out, scanning those attending the party, most of whom he recognized. Everyone was familiar, and he was beginning to grow discouraged.

"Merry's here, somewhere," he commented. "Or so I hope."

"She might be right before your eyes," Mary told him.

He doubted it. "Possible, but I don't think so. I'd recognize her if she was. I recognize everyone here so far."

"You think you'd recognize her?" she asked with a soft laugh that got his attention.

"I've never seen her, but I should be able to pick out an unfamiliar face."

"Perhaps she is familiar," Mary said.

"She implied as much; she said she knew me, which indicates that I'd know her." He'd spent countless hours wondering about that very thing and couldn't imagine how he knew her.

"Did you know HR misspelled my first name on the nameplate that was on my desk?" she asked him.

He blinked, finding it odd that she would mention this on her last day in the office.

"Did you tell HR?"

"Three times, but they didn't feel it was worth going to the trouble when I was a temp."

"I'm sorry. If you'd mentioned it earlier I would have made sure it was corrected." It was too late now, though.

"There's a reason I'm telling you this, Jayson. There's something you need to know . . ."

"I see her." Jayson exhaled quickly when he spotted the woman who came into the ballroom area. It had to be Merry, and she was gorgeous. His breath caught in his lungs. It **had** to be her. He knew every employee, and she was alone and walking purposefully toward him.

She was stunning. Stop-traffic gorgeous. She wore a red silk dress and heels, and the dress clung to her body in all the right places. And her body . . . wow, she was perfection. Her gaze zeroed in on him, and a small smile widened her mouth.

Automatically he stepped forward and held out his arm to her, welcoming her.

"Jayson," Mary said, touching his arm. "That can't be her."

Unable to take his eyes away from the beautiful woman walking directly toward him, Jayson didn't hear a word Mary said.

Merry was only a few feet away from him now. The closer she got, the more enraptured he became. She was a vision; her beauty took his breath away. Merry was far and away more than he'd ever anticipated or expected. What shocked him was that he didn't recognize her. He quickly scanned his thoughts, wondering where and when he might have seen her before, because she definitely wasn't someone he would forget.

"She's wearing my dress," Mary gulped.

That caught Jayson's attention. "What?"

Merry's brows rose to a perfect arch. "My dear, I can assure you that this is **my** dress."

Mary's face filled with a color that would rival Santa's suit. "I know, I apologize, it's just that I saw it in the store window and wanted it so badly." She snapped her mouth closed and then shot Jayson a mournful look. "She's beautiful. . . . I'll leave you two to become acquainted."

"Thank you," Merry said, smiling cordially at Mary.

"Here," Mary said, and handed Jayson a card. "Merry Christmas . . . I meant to leave this with the cookies, but I think it's best I didn't."

He took the card and Mary walked away.

As soon as Mary was out of sight, he turned to Merry and took her hand in both of his. "Merry. We meet at last."

"Merry?" she returned, smiling at him with perfectly white, even teeth. "My name isn't Merry. It's Sylvia. Sylvia De La Rosa. I'm the event planner you hired. I believe you're Jayson Bright, am I correct?"

"Your name isn't Merry?" He was too flustered to think clearly.

"No," she reiterated. "It's Sylvia. I thought I should introduce myself and ask if everything was to your satisfaction."

It took him an awkward moment before he could answer. "Yes, yes, it's perfectly fine."

"Good. We appreciate your business and hope that you'll consider using our company for other events."

"Of course," he said, doing his best to disguise his disappointment and embarrassment.

They shook hands and Sylvia left him to oversee the servers.

Once again, his eyes scanned the room. He couldn't find Merry anywhere.

Then it hit him, what Mary had said, and his head felt like it would explode.

It seemed out of context at the time, and he hadn't understood the significance of what she was trying to tell him.

Human Resources had misspelled her first name. Why in the name of heaven would she mention that to him now, at this party? Really, how many ways could you spell . . . his chest tightened.

Mary.

Merry.

Closing his eyes, his shoulders slumped forward as he groaned at his own stupidity.

Merry . . . **his** Merry had been right in front of him and he was too blind to see her. He fought back the urge to slap his forehead. He couldn't have been any denser.

She'd tried repeatedly to tell him and he hadn't heard her. A sick feeling attacked the pit of his stomach. Then Sylvia had appeared and he'd mistakenly assumed she was the woman he'd spent all those nights with chatting online. He couldn't imagine what Merry/Mary was thinking about him now. His groan grew louder.

This was a worse disaster than even he could imagine. He'd been swayed by a pretty face and ignored the beauty standing right next to him.

It all made sense now. Merry/Mary arrived at Starbucks and recognized him immediately. She didn't want anything to do with him. Prior to that, every time they had contact in the office it had been confrontational.

Still, there had been ample opportunity to explain who she was—that Mary and Merry were one and the same. And she hadn't done that. Instead, she'd strung him along. He was sorry for the way he'd acted, but she wasn't completely innocent in all of this. Furthermore, she owed him an explanation.

Jayson felt his breath freeze in his lungs, wanting to wipe out the entire night and start over. Good luck with that.

Without realizing what was happening,

he'd set himself up as the poster child for fool of the year.

But Mary/Merry also had to carry part of the blame. She should have told him who she was long ago; many opportunities had presented themselves.

Looking around, he didn't see her anywhere.

He started working his way through the crowd, weaving around couples until he saw a familiar face from the data-entry department.

"Kelly," he said, gripping the young woman by her shoulders.

"It's Kylie," she said.

"Kylie," he repeated. "Have you seen Merry?"

"Merry Knight?"

"Yes," he returned impatiently. "Merry Smith. Mary Knight. Whatever her name might be."

"She left."

CHAPTER FIFTEEN

✳

Merry

The entire evening couldn't have gone worse. Merry had all but told Jayson who she was and his focus had been on the woman in red who was gorgeous, tall, and graceful. She could have been a supermodel with the perfect body and perfect hair and makeup.

Perfect everything.

And Merry wasn't. No way could she compete against that. Furthermore, she wasn't going to try. If that model was the kind of woman Jayson wanted, the kind he was most attracted to, then this wasn't meant to be. That just wasn't her. Nor did she ever want to be.

Walking at a clipped pace out of the hotel, Merry couldn't get away from the party fast enough. The cold air hit her as she made her way down the street, her hands buried deep in her pockets.

Gradually, disappointment slowed her steps and she caught her breath. She bit into her lower lip, struggling to hold back the disappointment. She'd wanted this night to turn out so much better than it had.

Tears blurred her eyes and she quickly blinked them back. No way was she going to cry over him. She might not be competition for this supermodel, but she had nothing to be ashamed about.

"Merry."

She heard her name and recognized Jayson's voice. Choosing to ignore him, she picked up her pace and walked faster until she was practically trotting.

"Merry," he said again, his voice strong and unrelenting.

He sounded breathless, as if he'd jogged the entire way from the hotel. If he knew her better, he'd know it was best to leave her alone until she was ready to talk, and she was no way near ready.

Within a matter of seconds, he raced up alongside her. "We need to talk this out."

"Now isn't a good time."

"It's as good as any," he argued. "I want to know why you didn't tell me who you were earlier." His tight features demanded an explanation.

She didn't answer, which only seemed to frustrate him further.

"You had the perfect opportunity any number of times."

Her mouth remained closed and tight. She refused to look at him, staring down at the sidewalk instead.

"You played me."

That was too much. "I played **you**?" she cried. "It was circumstances, not something I planned deliberately. Think what you want, but you're completely off base. How could I have possibly known it was you until . . . never mind. It isn't important. Like I said, believe what you want."

"You're the one who refused to meet me."

She glared at him, unable to hold back any longer. "And you wonder why? You came across as arrogant and rude at work. I tried to cut ties, but you wouldn't let me. You were the one who said **please**."

"**Please?**" he demanded. "When did I say that?"

"You didn't say it. You typed it and . . . and then I gave in. My bad. Isn't that what you said? I knew then, and I should have listened to my gut because it would hurt a whole lot less now if I had."

"Did your coworkers know you were

playing me for an idiot? Was the entire company aware of your game?"

"Oh right. I told everyone," she said sarcastically. "I blabbed it to anyone who was willing to listen. Couldn't wait to make you a laughingstock. That's so like me."

His gaze narrowed into thin slits. "Did you, Merry? Did you purposely try to embarrass me?"

She could tell by his look that he wasn't sure if he should believe her or not.

She didn't want him to think she had set out to humiliate him. Hanging her head, she briefly closed her eyes. "No . . . no one knew."

He exhaled a harsh breath. "Thank you for that."

The fight left her as quickly as the anger came. "I'm sorry, Jay, sorrier than you know. I'm not the woman you want." If he'd been looking for someone like that beauty queen, then it would never be her. "I think it would be best if we forget about this whole fiasco."

He exhaled a deep breath, glanced toward the sky, and then slowly nodded.

Her heart felt like it was going to break in half. She had no one to blame but herself. She'd known the moment she saw him sitting in Starbucks holding that bouquet of daisies that they were all wrong for each other.

"I guess there's nothing more to say, then," she murmured.

He nodded. "I am curious about one thing."

She looked up at him, struggling to hide the pain pounding in her chest. "What?"

"This." He caught her by her shoulders and brought his mouth down to hers. His lips were cold against her own. Catching her by surprise, she wasn't sure what was happening and why he would want to kiss her, especially now that she was ready to walk away entirely and be done with this entire mess.

Once the shock left her, she found herself opening to him. Rising on the tips of her toes, her arms circled his neck and she gave herself over to this kiss. He tasted wonderful, a mixture of champagne and desire. His kiss was everything she remembered.

And so much more.

She wasn't sure how long they continued to kiss. Not until someone shouted a catcall in their direction did they stop. He pushed her away and stared at her for several seconds. Neither of them seemed capable of speech.

Merry raised her fingertips to her lips while keeping his gaze, holding on to the wonder of his kiss, although that was impossible. "Do you have your answer?"

He nodded.

And with that, he turned his back to her and walked away.

CHAPTER SIXTEEN

✳

Jayson

Jayson couldn't get away fast enough. As he headed down the street, he mused that it would have been far better if he hadn't kissed Merry again. But he had and now his head and his heart were filled with the taste of her. All it had done was create a craving for more.

Her contract had ended, so he wouldn't see her at the office again, which was good, as that would have been awkward. For all intents and purposes, she was out of his life. It was better that way.

Instead of returning to the Christmas

party, Jayson headed home, discouraged and depressed. He'd had high hopes for Merry and him. High hopes that had come crashing down with the speed of a misfired rocket.

The doorman greeted him with a smile, which quickly faded when he saw the look on Jayson's face. Not wanting to ruin anyone else's evening, Jayson raised his hand, acknowledging the other man. It was then that he noticed the homeless man sitting at the corner.

The doorman's gaze followed Jayson's. "I've notified the authorities and he leaves, but then the next day he's back."

Jayson walked over to the man, who looked up at him with determination. "I ain't moving. You can call the cops if you want, but this is a public sidewalk."

Jayson didn't argue. "You have a name?"

"What do you want to know for?"

"I'm Jayson."

"You were with that girl who gave me the chocolate cake?"

Jayson nodded. "That's me." Reaching inside his three-quarter-length raincoat, he pulled out his wallet and removed a hundred-dollar bill. "Merry Christmas," he said.

The homeless man looked at him like he was dreaming. "You sure you want me to have that?"

"I'm sure."

"Name's Billy."

"Merry Christmas, Billy." He headed into the building where it was warm and beautifully decorated for the holidays with lights and a large Christmas tree. Merry and bright.

"Merry Christmas, Jayson," Billy called after him.

Peter, the doorman, stared at him like he didn't recognize Jayson, but he didn't say anything.

Jayson rode the elevator to his condo. The inside was cold and dark by contrast. He had no decorations. No holiday display of any kind. It felt stark and bare. His life felt the same.

As was his habit, he walked over to the wine rack and poured himself a glass of wine. He left the lights off and sagged down onto his sofa, staring into the night with the festive lights below. It'd started to snow and he glanced at his wrist, checking the time. Thirty-five minutes after the hour. Merry would be on the bus. He could see her sitting by the window, looking out at the falling snow. He wondered what her thoughts were or if she was as disheartened and disappointed as he was.

What a major debacle their relationship had turned out to be. To think he'd known Merry all along. He should have figured it out. How unbelievably dense he'd been. She'd practically told him outright who she was. The comment about the woman he was looking to meet being right in front of him, and later how HR had misspelled her first name. What a dunce!

Reaching for his phone, he pushed the button that would connect him with Cooper. His cousin answered on the second ring, and Jayson could hear festive music in the background.

"Hey, did your long-lost love finally show?"

"Yeah."

The teasing quality immediately left Cooper's voice. "What happened?"

"Where are you?" Jayson asked instead.

"Doesn't matter."

"Cooper!"

"I'm with Maddy and her family. Now tell me what happened, and it doesn't sound like it was good, if what I'm hearing in your voice is any indication."

Jayson had no intention of denying it. "Remember how I told you she said she knew me?"

"Yeah, so?"

"So, to make a long story short, Merry is Mary."

"Say that again."

Jayson had hoped his cousin would catch on right away. "M-A-R-Y and M-E-R-R-Y are one and the same."

"Merry and Mary are the same person?" Cooper exhaled as he took in the significance of what Jayson had said. "Wow, bet that was a shocker."

"It was. I should have guessed sooner. I blew it, Cooper. Blew it big-time. Saw someone else and thought it was her. It wasn't. Mary was trying to tell me she was M-E-R-R-Y but I was distracted by someone else who I **thought** was Merry. When I realized what she'd been trying to tell me, I got angry, thinking she played me for a fool."

"Did she?"

"Don't know. In retrospect, I doubt that she did."

"You like her? Both Merry and Mary?"

He wasn't sure how to answer. "I don't know what to think. Thought it was best to end it, walk away. She suggested it and I agreed, but I did something utterly stupid."

"What?"

"I kissed her."

His words were met with silence and then, "How was it?"

"On a scale of one to ten, it was about a hundred."

Jayson knew the minute he'd walked away how badly he wanted Merry. The background music faded slightly, which told Jayson his cousin had walked out of the room. He didn't want to disrupt his cousin's holiday celebration. "Listen, Cooper, you're in the middle of a party. I'll catch up with you later."

"Don't be a fool, Jay. If you care about this woman, then do something about it."

"Right." The problem was he didn't

know where to start. Merry wanted nothing more to do with him. The entire situation was a disaster. His initial reaction was to end it all, but the choice had been hers. At this point, he could only do so much, and he felt like he had to abide by her wishes.

Cooper continued talking, offering Jayson friendly advice, most of which faded into silence, lost on him. When he didn't respond, his cousin suggested Jayson sleep on it and call him in the morning and they'd talk some more.

Jayson agreed but suspected there would be no sleep on his part. It felt like a lead weight had landed on his chest, paralyzing him.

After a second glass of wine, Jayson grew sleepy. He rarely drank more than two glasses. It was only nine-thirty, too early to go to bed. Leaning his head back against the couch, he closed his eyes. That was a mistake, because the minute he did, Merry's image took shape in his mind, her fingertips pressed to her lips, looking up at him with eyes that made him want to do nothing more than kiss her again and again.

He couldn't have bungled the situation any worse. How could he have mistaken the event planner for Merry when the beautiful woman he'd fallen in love with stood right in front of him? His initial reaction was to assume Merry had played him for a fool. He was a fool, all right, one of his own making.

Thinking she might have had a change of heart, he felt a surge of energy and stepped into his home office and logged on to his computer. His heart swelled when he saw there was a message from her. He immediately clicked on it.

You hurt my sister.

Patrick.

I don't like you anymore, and neither does she.

Reading this was only torturing himself. Anyone with half a brain would disconnect and leave matters as they were. Not Jayson. He was looking for punishment and so he continued to read.

Merry is in her room and she won't talk to me or my mom and dad.

After spilling his guts to his cousin, he wasn't in the mood to talk much, either.

You ruined my sister's Christmas, and she's a good person. Why would you do that? Why would you hurt her feelings? I liked you and Mom liked you, too, and even my dad liked you. We were all happy that she was going to meet you and then she came home and wouldn't talk to anyone. What did you do? What did you say? Tell me, because Merry won't say anything.

His heart sank as he struggled with how to make this right and realized it wasn't possible. The best he could do was wait until after the holidays and find a way to build a bridge.

This is going to be the worst Christmas ever. Merry is sad and now Mom thinks we did the wrong thing and it's all your fault. I hope you have a crummy Christmas. Patrick.

Jayson could guarantee that he was going to have a miserable Christmas. It had never bothered him before. Christmas had no real meaning for him. It never had. The best he could do was have dinner with his uncle and they would discuss business. A restaurant meal.

Heaving a sigh, he closed his laptop and headed into his room for a shower. It felt as if he carried the weight of the world on his shoulders.

Merry Christmas. His would be without the Merry for sure.

CHAPTER SEVENTEEN

✳

Merry

Merry spent a sleepless night. When she emerged from her bedroom on the morning of Christmas Eve, she saw the worried look her parents sent her way. Patrick, too.

"Are you ready to tell us what happened when you finally met Jayson?" her mother asked, her face tender and concerned.

Pouring herself a cup of coffee, Merry debated how much to say. After her first sip, she managed to offer those she loved most a reassuring smile. "The meeting between Jay and me didn't go as well as

I'd hoped." That said it all and so much more. She'd rather not go into lengthy explanations. As much as possible, she wanted to put last evening out of her mind.

"From your reaction when you arrived home last night, that was pretty much our assumption," her mother surmised.

Merry realized she would need to explain a bit more. "Jayson . . . was upset and thought I'd played him for a fool."

"Oh Merry," her mother whispered sympathetically. "Surely you told him that was never the case."

"I tried, but I don't think he believed me."

"Did you give Jayson the cookies we baked?" Patrick asked and reached for his hot cocoa.

She nodded. "I left them on his desk at the office."

"Take them back."

"Patrick," their mother chastised, "they were a gift. We'd never take them back." She returned her attention to Merry. "Now tell us about your last day at the office."

"It was great. Lauren and Kylie brought in a cake and we celebrated together. I'm going to miss them."

"If you're not working for Jayson, it will make all this easier," her mother commented.

"I thought of that, too. It would be agony to see him every day." It went without saying that Jayson would have no desire to see her.

"I hate to see you upset," her mother said. "I know this meeting was a big disappointment. I feel bad. Your brother and I were the ones who involved you in all this. I hope you know our intentions were good."

"Mom, please." Merry walked over

to where her mother sat at the kitchen table and wrapped her arms around Robin's shoulders and kissed her temple. "I wouldn't have missed this for the world. Jay will always hold a tender spot in my heart. I don't have a single regret."

"You don't hate him?" Patrick demanded.

"I could never hate Jay," she said, and remembered the beautiful kiss they'd shared. She would always remember his kisses.

"But he hurt your feelings," Patrick said, interrupting her thoughts.

"I'm disappointed, yes, but I think Jay was genuinely disappointed, too. It happens that way sometimes. I should have known better than to involve my heart, but like I said, I don't regret a single minute. I'm grateful because Jay helped me to appreciate how blessed I am with all of you." Jay had never known the love of a close-knit family the way she had; he'd never experienced a real Christmas.

"Do you think he liked you, too?" Patrick asked next.

That question required some thought. After all the nights spent online, opening their lives and their hearts to each other, she had to believe that he did hold some tender feelings for her. He couldn't have faked that. Nor could she. "In his own way, I believe he liked Merry. It was the other woman who confuses him."

"What other woman?" Patrick wanted to know, cocking his head to one side to understand.

"The Mary who worked in his office."

"But that's you." Patrick shook his head as if that would help him understand.

"I know. It's rather confusing."

"Is Jay confused?" Patrick asked.

"I don't think Jay is, but Jayson definitely is."

Patrick looked at her long and hard and she could almost see the wheels in his mind spinning. "But isn't Jay Jayson?"

She nodded rather than go into a lengthy explanation. "Like I said, it's a big muddled mess to him, to me, and to just about everyone else."

"It's Christmas Eve," her mother reminded them all. "No sad faces are allowed. I have a turkey in the refrigerator and we're going to stuff that bird and cook him into the finest Christmas dinner we've ever had."

"You bought a turkey?" Patrick was thrilled. "I like turkey."

"You like everything," Merry reminded him, kissing him on the top of the head. "What can I do to help, Mom?" she asked, determined not to let her hurting heart dampen the family's Christmas spirit.

Her mother locked eyes with Merry, seemingly aware of her daughter's effort to make the best of the situation. "I'd like to get as much of the food preparation done today so we won't be spending all our time in the kitchen tomorrow."

"Good idea." The busier Merry was, the less time she'd have to think about Jayson and the mess she'd made. She'd put off thoughts of him until later, when she felt better prepared to deal with the myriad of emotions that churned inside of her.

Well, she could try.

Her mother had a list of tasks that kept Merry busy until mid-morning. Her father was out and about, and it wasn't until noon before she realized her brother had been quiet all morning. He almost always enjoyed helping in the kitchen, too.

"Where's Patrick?" Merry asked, her suspicions rising.

Her mother was busy at the kitchen table, peeling potatoes, and glanced up. "The last time I saw him he was playing computer games."

That made sense, seeing that Merry had dominated the family computer for weeks now. The only time Patrick had to play his computer games was right after school.

"Lunch is ready. I'll get him."

Merry sought out her brother and found him sitting on his bed with the computer on his lap. "Patrick?"

He glanced up and his eyes widened with a look of surprise and guilt.

Merry knew that look all too well. "What are you doing, Patrick?" she asked, stepping farther into his bedroom.

He closed the computer and shook his head adamantly. "Nothing."

"It doesn't look like nothing to me." A sickening feeling attacked her stomach. "Were you online with Jay?"

Her brother's eyes bulged and again he adamantly shook his head. "I promised not to tell."

"Patrick." She groaned and sank onto

the bed next to her brother. "What did you do?"

"He made me promise not to tell."

"What did you tell him?" she pleaded. "Please, Patrick, I need to know."

He stared at her for a long time. "You promise not to be mad at me?"

She wasn't sure she could swear to it. "I'll do my best."

"I told him you were sad. I was mad at him, too, and told him I wanted him to have a crummy Christmas, but then I felt bad and told him I changed my mind and he could have a good Christmas and I was sorry I said all those things to him."

Merry sat down on the bed next to her brother. "I'm glad you apologized."

"I . . . I told him what you said," he added evasively.

"Which was what? Remember, I said a lot of things."

The guilty look returned and he avoided eye contact. "Just that you had no regrets and that you couldn't be angry with him. You said that, right?"

Her chest tightened before she nodded. These were words she'd prefer he hadn't shared. Rather than berate her brother who only meant well, she reminded him it was time for lunch.

"Did you make toasted cheese sandwiches?" Patrick asked. Those were his favorite, along with peanut butter and jelly.

"I believe I did," she said, hugging her brother. She wasn't entirely sure what Patrick had said to Jayson. "Will you do me a favor?" she asked as she looped an arm over his shoulder. "Don't write to Jay again, okay?"

Her brother sighed expressively. "Never?"

"Please," she whispered, her throat tight and raw.

"I'll do my best," he said, repeating her own promise to him earlier.

Her mother tired out easily and laid down to rest following lunch. Merry was cleaning the kitchen when the doorbell rang. Bogie barked and raced across the living room, while Patrick leaped from the kitchen table and rushed to the front door. Bogie raced to the door with him, tail wagging.

With a dish towel slung over her shoulder, Merry followed her brother.

Patrick opened the door and Jayson walked into the house. Bogie barked furiously, slapping his tail against his legs in eagerness to greet him. Jayson petted him, which Bogie loved, and then Bogie dutifully returned to his bed.

Merry gasped, sucking in a deep breath.

His gaze instantly locked with hers. "Merry Christmas."

"What . . ." She fumbled with words, hardly knowing where to start. She meant to ask him what he was doing. Instead, she stood looking at him, her mouth hanging open and her voice completely lost.

He looked good, as if he'd slept like a baby, while she'd spent a miserable night staring up at the ceiling, wondering what she could have done, should have done, differently. She wanted to ask him that very question. Instead, she stood rooted to the floor, hardly able to breathe, just looking at him.

Her mother was in the recliner and woke, opening her eyes. She blinked a couple times and then smiled. "You must be Jayson Bright."

"I am." Jay stepped forward and gently took her mother's hand.

"I believe you're here for my daughter," her father said, standing to greet him.

"I am," he answered, his gaze wavering briefly away from Merry.

"He's here for me, too," Patrick insisted. "I invited him. Mom said I could."

"Mom?" Merry asked, unable to hide her surprise.

"I believe we should give Merry and Mr. Bright a few minutes alone," her mother told Patrick. "You okay with that?"

Patrick nodded, but Merry sensed his reluctance.

She retreated into the kitchen and Jayson followed her. She stood with her back against the counter, fearing her heart was in her eyes for him to read. He simply took her breath away and so she waited for him to speak first.

"You feel any different this morning?" he asked.

She swallowed against the lump in her throat. "Different about us, you mean?"

He shrugged. "I'm here to ask if you're willing to give us a shot? I want to apologize for the things I said yesterday. I wasn't thinking clearly. Here you were standing right in front me, doing your best to tell me who you were. Instead of listening, I had my eye on another woman, certain she was the one I'd been longing to meet."

"She was beautiful, and sophisticated and graceful—"

"But she wasn't you," he said, cutting her off. "You're the woman I want, Merry, and you're beautiful, both inside and out. That event planner might have been attractive, but she isn't you, and you . . . you mean the world to me."

Merry's eyes welled, but she refused to let the tears come.

"You are the most amazing woman I've ever known, Merry Knight, and I'm crazy about you and that dimple of yours."

"My dimple."

"Fell in love with it the first time I saw it."

"Oh. And when was that?"

He grinned. "I saw you eating lunch at your desk, which is . . ."

". . . against company policy," she finished for him.

"I stared you down and you didn't flinch, but that dimple appeared. Ever since that day I've wanted to kiss it in the worst way."

"That's not true."

"Maybe not then, but it is now." His grin widened. "It's out in full force right now."

She raised her hand to her cheek as if to confirm what he said.

He exhaled slowly. "After I left you at the bus stop last night, I went home to an empty, cold condo and realized something important."

"Oh."

"It was dark there even with the lamp on. Even with the city below in full holiday display. You're the light in my life, Merry. You have my heart. When my cousin told me he was marrying Maddy, a girl we'd both known years ago, he told me he just knew that she was the one for him. He wasn't going to take a chance on losing her. At the time, I had trouble not rolling my eyes.

"I understand what he meant now. You're the one for me, Merry. I know if I let pride stand between us that it could possibly be the biggest mistake of my life, and I'm not willing to risk that. So," he said, and breathed deeply, "I'm asking if you're willing to give me another chance."

Her heart melted at his words, and despite what he said, she had trouble believing it was really her he wanted. "But . . . you saw the woman in red and you wanted her . . ."

"Wanted her? No way. I was a fool not to recognize what was right in front of my eyes. I'm so sorry about that, Merry. My name might be Bright, but until I met you I was lost in a black void. You were the one who showed me the way out of the dark. You're the one who showed me I was **in** the dark."

He stepped toward her and she met

him halfway. He pulled Merry into his arms and hugged her close, as if she were the most precious gift he'd ever received. "I knew the minute I held you we were meant to be together. And those kisses we shared. Tell me you felt it, too?"

She nodded, because she, too, had experienced that sense of rightness. She felt at home in his arms.

"I knew it," he whispered and kissed her again, his mouth warm and eager over hers. Merry wrapped herself around him, holding on to him as if she never wanted to let him go.

"Mom, Mom," Patrick cried out from the hallway. "They're kissing. That's a good sign, right?"

"A very good sign," Merry heard her mother reply. "I'd say the future looks merry and bright," she said, calling out from the kitchen.

"That's funny, Mom," Patrick said, laughing.

Jayson Bright broke off the kiss and Merry smiled up at him. Leaning up on her tiptoes, she pressed her forehead against his.

"I'll never look at Christmas the same way again," he whispered close to her ear. "Not as long as I've got you in my life."

Patrick stuck his head around the corner and whispered back to his mother, "They're kissing again."

"Patrick, please," Merry warned. "Jay and I would like some privacy."

Her brother cast his gaze to the floor. "I wanted to know that Mom and I did the right thing."

"You did," she assured him, smiling up at Jayson. "You couldn't have chosen better."

"I'm the lucky one," Jayson insisted, wrapping his arms around Merry, holding her close. He kissed her again and then broke away and looked at her brother.

"Say, Patrick, could you give me a hand."

Ever eager to help, Patrick leaped up and followed Jayson outside to where he'd parked his car. Together the two of them carted in beautifully wrapped gifts to set under the tree, and then Jayson returned for a second load while Merry looked on, unable to believe her eyes.

Merry and her parents watched in stunned disbelief when Jay returned with a large box, which he set on the kitchen counter. Merry glanced inside and noticed a prime rib roast.

"I was going to invite myself to dinner," Jayson explained when she cast a curious look in his direction. "It seemed rude not to make a contribution toward the meal."

Sorting through the contents of the box, Merry noticed he'd provided an entire four-course dinner fit for royalty. "We were going to order pizza tonight . . ."

"Prime rib," her father broke in. "Merry, we're having prime rib. I think we can forgo the pizza."

"The roast is cooked and ready to eat. All that's needed is for everything to be heated."

"Jayson, oh my," Robin whispered, seemingly overwhelmed, her hands close to her mouth. "This is too much."

"I wanted to thank you and Patrick for signing Merry up on Mix & Mingle, and Bogie, too—"

"Mom, Dad, look," Patrick cried out, interrupting Jayson. Her brother sat next to the Christmas tree, crumpled Christmas wrap at his feet, holding a laptop computer. "Jayson got me my own laptop."

"Patrick, you're supposed to wait until Christmas," his father chastised.

"I know, I know, but it was a big package and it had my name on it."

"Oh Jayson," Merry whispered, her

eyes clouding with tears. She knew how badly her brother wanted his own computer. "That's perfect."

He wrapped his arm around her waist as though being separated from her longer than a few minutes was too long. "The only thing that feels perfect is being with you and your family," he whispered.

"We don't need gifts as long as I've got you."

"You've got me," Jayson said. "My cousin told me I'd know when I'd found the right woman, and I do."

"I know, too," she whispered back. And she did.

Savor the magic of the season with
Debbie Macomber's Christmas novel

Twelve Days of Christmas

Filled with warmth, humor, and the
promise of love.
Continue reading for a preview.

Available from Ballantine Books.

CHAPTER ONE

✳

Cain Maddox stepped into the elevator, and then just as the doors were about to close he heard a woman call out.

"Hold that for me."

Cain thrust out his arm to keep the doors from sliding shut. He inwardly groaned when he saw the woman who lived across the hall come racing toward him. He kept his eyes trained straight ahead, not inviting conversation. He'd run into this particular woman several times in the last few months since he'd moved into the building. She'd stopped several times to pet Schroeder, his Irish setter. The one he'd inherited from his grandfather when Bernie had moved into the assisted-living complex. She'd chattered away, lavishing affection on the dog. Not the talkative type, Cain responded minimally to her questions. He liked her all right, but she was a bit much, over the top with that cutesy smile. Okay, he'd admit it. He found her attractive. He wasn't sure what it was about her, because usually the chirpy, happy ones didn't appeal to him. Regardless, nothing would come of it, and that suited him. He knew better. Yet every time he saw her a yellow light started flashing in his head. **Warning, warning. Danger ahead.** Cain could feel this woman was trouble the first moment he saw her and heard her exuberant "good morning." Even her name was cheerful: Julia. Looking at her, it was easy to envision the opening scene from **The Sound of Music,** with Julie Andrews twirling around, arms extended, singing, joyful, excited. Even the thought was enough to make Cain cringe. He could do happy, just not first thing in the morning.

To put it simply, he found little good about mornings, and second, he'd learned a long time ago not to trust women, especially the types who were enthusiastic and friendly. Experience had taught him well, and, having been burned once, he wasn't eager to repeat the experience.

"Thanks," she said a bit breathlessly as she floated into the elevator. Yes, floated. Her coat swirled around her as she came to stand beside him. On her coat's lapel she wore a pretty Christmas-tree pin that sparkled with jewel-tone stones. "I'm running late this morning."

Pushing the button to close the door, Cain ignored her. He didn't mean to be rude, but he wasn't up for conversation.

"Didn't I see you walking Schroeder in the dog park the other day?" she asked.

"No." He hadn't seen her. Maybe he had, but he wasn't willing to admit it.

"Really? I'm pretty sure I saw you."

He let her comment fall into empty space. Could this elevator move any slower?

Fortunately, the elevator arrived at the foyer before she could continue the conversation.

"You aren't much of a morning person, are you?" she asked as he collected his newspaper, tucked it under his arm, and headed for the door.

Julia reached for her own and followed him. Would he never shake this woman? They were welcomed by the Seattle drizzle that was part of the winter norm for the Pacific Northwest. Cain's office at the insurance company where he worked as an actuary was within easy walking distance. Julia matched her steps with his until she reached the bus stop outside the Starbucks, where, thankfully, she stopped.

"Have a good day," she called after him.

Cain would, especially now that he was free of Ms. Sunshine.

"Excuse me?" Julia Padden stood in the foyer of her apartment building the following morning, astonished that her neighbor would steal her newspaper while she stood directly in front of him. She braced her fist against her hip and raised both her finely shaped eyebrows at him.

Showing his displeasure, Cain Maddox turned to face her, newspaper in hand. He had to be the most unpleasant human being she'd ever met. She'd tried the friendly route and got the message. Even his dog had better manners than he did.

"I believe that newspaper is mine." Her

apartment number had been clearly written with a bold Sharpie over the plastic wrapper. This was no innocent mistake. For whatever reason, Cain had taken a disliking to her. Well, fine, she could deal with that, but she wasn't about to let him walk all over her, and she wasn't going to stand idly by and let him steal from her, either.

At the sound of her voice, Cain looked up.

Irritated and more than a little annoyed, Julia thrust out her hand, palm up. "My newspaper, please."

To her astonishment, he hesitated. Oh puleese! She'd caught him red-handed in the act and he had the nerve to look irritated **at her.** How typical. Not only was he reluctant to return it, but he didn't have the common decency to look the least bit guilty. She'd say one thing about him . . . the man had nerve.

"Someone took mine," he explained, as if that gave him the right to steal hers. "Take someone else's. It doesn't matter if it's technically yours or not."

"It most certainly does; it matters to me." To prove her point, she jerked her hand at him a second time. "I am not taking someone else's newspaper and you most certainly aren't taking mine. Now give it to me."

"Okay, fine." He slapped the newspaper into her open palm, then reached over and snagged some other unsuspecting apartment owner's.

Julia's jaw sagged open. "I can't believe you did that."

He rolled his eyes, tucked the newspaper under his arm, and headed toward the revolving door, briefcase in hand.

This wasn't the first time her morning paper had mysteriously disappeared, either, and now she knew who was responsible. Not only was Cain Maddox unfriendly, he was a thief. Briefly she wondered what else he might be responsible for taking. And this close to Christmas, too, the season of goodwill and charity. Of course theft was wrong at any time of the year, but resorting to it during the holidays made it downright immoral. Apparently, her grumpy neighbor hadn't taken the spirit of Christmas to heart.

That shouldn't surprise her.

Cain and Julia often left for work close to the same time in the morning. Three times this week they'd inadvertently met at the elevator. Being a morning person and naturally cheerful, Julia always greeted him with a sunny smile and a warm "good morning." The most response she'd gotten out of him was a terse nod. Mostly he ignored her, as if he hadn't heard her speak.

Julia waited until she was on the bus

before she called her best friend, Cammie Nightingale, who now lived outside of Denver. They'd attended college together. Cammie had graduated ahead of her when Julia's finances had dried up and she'd been forced to take night classes and work full-time. After seeing so many of her friends struggling to pay off student loans, Julia had opted to avoid the financial struggles. Yes, it took her longer to get her degree in communications, and no, she hadn't found the job of her dreams, but she was close, so close. Furthermore, she was debt-free. Currently she worked at Macy's department store, where she'd been employed for the last seven years.

"You won't believe what happened this morning," she said as soon as Cammie picked up. Her friend was married and had a two-year-old and a newborn.

"Hold on a minute," Cammie said.

In her irritation, Julia hadn't asked if Cammie could talk. She waited a couple minutes before her friend picked up again.

"What's going on?"

"My disagreeable neighbor, the one I told you about, is a thief. He tried to steal my newspaper."

"He didn't?"

"I caught him red-handed, and when I confronted him and demanded he give it back he took someone else's."

"What? You're kidding me."

"No joke. Not only that, he was rude **again**." Come to think of it, he'd never been anything but unfriendly. It was men like him who put a damper on Christmas. Julia refused to let him or anyone else spoil her holidays.

"Are you talking about the guy who lives across the hall from you?"

"The very one." The more Julia thought

about what he'd done, the more upset she got. Okay, so he wasn't a morning person. She could deal with that. But to steal her newspaper? That was low.

"What do you know about him?" Cammie asked.

"Nothing . . . well, other than he has a gorgeous Irish setter that he walks every morning." She'd tried being neighborly, but Cain had let it be known he wasn't interested. She'd started more than one conversation only to be subtly and not so subtly informed he took exception to small talk. After several such attempts, she got the message.

"Maybe he's shy."

Cammie possessed a generous spirit, but this time she was wrong. Anyone who'd take her newspaper without a shred of guilt wasn't shy. "I doubt it. Trust me on this. Cain Maddox isn't shy, and furthermore, he's not to be trusted."

"You don't know that."

"You're wrong. I have this gift, a sixth sense about men. This one is sinister."

Cammie's laughter filled the phone. "Sinister? Come on, Julia."

"I'm serious," she insisted. "Just what kind of man steals a newspaper? I don't know what I ever did to offend him, but he's made it more than clear he would rather kiss a snake than have anything to do with me." That bothered Julia more than she was comfortable admitting. He was kinda cute, too, in a stiff sort of way. He was tall, a good six or seven inches above her own five-foot-five frame.

His hair was dark and cut in a way that said he was a professional. The shape of his jaw indicated he had a stubborn bent, but that could be conjecture on her part, based on what she knew about him. And as best she could tell, he didn't possess a single laugh line, although he did have beautiful, clear dark chocolate eyes.

The only time she'd seen him in anything but a suit was when he was at the dog park. He wore a jacket with the name of an insurance company and logo, which she assumed he was connected to in some way, and jeans. Even then he didn't look relaxed, and he held himself away from others.

"Are you attracted to him?" Cammie asked.

"You've got to be kidding me. No way!"

"I have a feeling this is why you're thirty-one and not in a serious relationship. How long are you going to hold on to Dylan, Julia?"

"That again?" Julia didn't have time for relationships and she for sure wasn't going to drag Dylan into the conversation. She was over him and had been for a long time. The problem was she had no time to date, between working and volunteering at church and for the Boys and Girls Club. Cammie knew that.

Besides, she had more important matters on her mind.

The blog. The challenge.

She'd gone through two intense interviews at Harvestware, a major software company, and the list had been narrowed down to two people. Because the job was in social media, the company had suggested a competition between the two candidates in the form of a blog. The one who could generate the largest following in the month of December would be awarded the job.

Julia had gladly accepted the challenge. Unfortunately, she hadn't had a lot of success so far; her following was minimal at best. This was her chance to prove herself.

"Maybe your neighbor is the man of your dreams."

"Cain Maddox? He's cold, Cammie. You haven't seen him. I have. Trust me—

he's not the kind of man you'd want to meet in a dark alley."

The more Julia thought about it, the more convinced she became that her neighbor was some disreputable character. A chill went down her spine just thinking about the cold look in his eyes.

Cammie laughed out loud. "Your creative imagination is getting away from you, my friend."

"Maybe, but I doubt it."

"Julia," her friend said in that calm way of hers that suggested Julia was overreacting. "He took your newspaper; he didn't threaten to bury you in concrete."

"It's the look in his eyes, like he sees straight through people."

"You've noticed his eyes?"

"Yes, they're brown and dark. Really dark and distant." Okay, Cammie was probably right. To see him in criminal terms was a bit of a stretch, but Julia wasn't exactly having warm, cozy feelings toward her neighbor.

"If that's the case, then I think you should kill him," Cammie suggested.

Julia gasped. She couldn't believe her bestie would even hint at such a thing.

"Kill him with kindness," Cammie elaborated.

"This guy needs a whole lot more than kindness." Leave it to her tenderhearted friend to suggest something sweet and good.

"It's twelve days until Christmas," she added after a moment, sounding excited.

"Yes. So?"

"This is it, Julia. You've been wanting an idea that would generate interest in your blog. Your neighbor is the perfect subject." Cammie seemed to be growing more enthused by the second. "Weren't you saying just the other day how you were desperate for an over-the-top idea?"

"Well, yes, but . . ."

"This is perfect," Cammie continued. "Kill him with kindness on your blog and report your progress for the next twelve days."

Julia wasn't keen on this. The less exposure to Cain Maddox she had, the better. "I don't know . . ."

"The countdown is sure to attract attention to your blog. All you need to do is to be kind to him. You're naturally friendly and funny. This guy won't know what hit him. And then you can document what happens on your blog. Mark my words, readers will love this."

"Did you even hear what I said?" Julia reminded her friend. "I can tell you right now kindness isn't going to affect him one way or the other."

"You won't know until you try."

Julia bit down on her lower lip as visions of winning that highly paid position swirled in her head. Maybe Cammie was right. Maybe this idea would be just what she needed to generate a following that would show off her communication and writing skills.

"I think people are responding to my blog about Christmas decorations."

"Julia, do you have any idea how many people blog about making homemade tree ornaments? You're no Martha Stewart. You need something fresh and fun. A subject that will pique interest, something different—and frankly, wreath-making isn't it."

Surely there was a better way to tackle this challenge. Showing kindness to someone she disliked wouldn't be easy. In addition, she sincerely doubted it would make any difference. The man was annoying, disagreeable, and stubborn.

"You aren't saying anything," Cammie said, interrupting her thoughts. "Which, from experience, I know is a good sign. You're actually considering doing this, aren't you?"

Bouncing her index finger against her mouth, Julia said, "I suppose killing him with kindness is worth a try."

"It totally is. And you can title your blog 'Twelve Days of Christmas.' "

Truthfully, Julia wasn't convinced this would work.

Cammie had no reservations, though. "It could inspire an entire movement."

"I'll give it some thought."

"Good. Gotta scoot. Scottie's eating the cat's food again."

Julia smiled as she disconnected, picturing the toddler eagerly stuffing cat food into his mouth while his mother was sidetracked on the phone. Cammie was a great ideas person, and Julia appreciated her friend's insight.

Bottom line: Julia didn't know how much longer she could hold out working in menswear at Macy's. The holidays were the most challenging. Her hours were long and she was required to work in the wee hours of the morning on Black Friday, which meant she hadn't been able to fly home for Thanksgiving.

Spending time with her family over Christmas looked to be a bust, too. Her parents would have been happy to pay for her airfare, but at thirty-one, Julia didn't feel she should rely on them to pick up the expense. Besides, she had commitments.

As her church's pianist, she was needed to accompany the choir. The talented singing group had scheduled a few special appearances, the last of which was coming up this weekend. She was grateful her boss had agreed to let her schedule her hours around those obligations. In addition, Julia was a volunteer for the holiday program at the Boys and Girls Club.

The bus continued to plug along as her thoughts spun with ideas. Julia gazed out the window, admiring the lights and the window displays along the short route that would take her to the very heart of downtown Seattle. She really did love the holidays. It was a special time of year.

Maybe she could treat Cain Maddox's surly mood with extra doses of nice. It would be an interesting test of the power of kindness. As a bonus, she wouldn't need to stress about content for her blog. She would simply be reporting the results. Easy-peasy.

But being impulsive had gotten her into trouble before, and so Julia decided to mull it over before making a final decision.

By the time she returned to her apartment that evening, it was dark and miserable, with drizzling rain and heavy traffic. Her feet hurt and she was exhausted. These long holiday hours at the store were killers.

Killers. Hmm . . . her mind automatically went to her neighbor. Killing him with kindness. It was a shame that Cain Maddox was such a killjoy.

Not wanting to fuss with dinner, she heated a can of soup and ate it with her feet propped up in front of the television. She caught the last of the local news broadcast. The weatherman forecasted more drizzle.

In the mood for something to lift her spirits, she turned off the television and reached for her phone. A little music was sure to do that. Besides, it would be good to familiarize herself with the songs for the performance coming up this weekend. Scrolling down her playlist, she chose a few classic Christmas carols, the ones the senior citizens seemed to enjoy the most at the choir's last performance at an assisted-living complex.

Julia sang along with the music as she washed the few dishes she'd dirtied and tidied her apartment. Music had always soothed her. She sang loudly through her personal favorites: "Silent Night." "O Little Town of Bethlehem." "It Came upon a Midnight Clear."

She was just about to belt out "Joy to the World" when someone pounded against her door. The knock was sharp and impatient. Determined.

Oh dear. Julia hoped her singing hadn't disturbed anyone.

She opened the door wearing an apologetic smile and was confronted by her nemesis from across the hall. Cain Maddox. She should have known.

His eyes snapped with irritation.

"What can I do for you?" she asked, doing her best to remain pleasant.

He continued to glare at her, his scowl darkening his already shady eyes. It was a shame, too—he was an attractive man, or he could be if he wasn't constantly frowning. She noticed he had a high forehead above a shapely mouth. Her father claimed a high forehead was a sign of intelligence, which was ridiculous. The only reason he said that was because his forehead was high. The thought caused her to smile.

"Is anyone dying in here? Because that's what it sounds like."

Holding her temper was a challenge. "Are you referring to my singing?"

"Tone. It. Down."

Not please, not thank you, just a demand.

With one hand still on her apartment door, Julia met his stare. "It's music. Christmas music, to be precise."

"I know what it is," he said with a groan, and briefly slammed his eyes shut.

"Would I be wrong to suggest that a kind, gentle soul such as yourself objects to a few classic Christmas carols?" she asked, ever so sweetly. Her words flowed like warm honey.

He glared at her as if she'd spoken in

a foreign language. "All I ask is that you cut the racket."

"Please," she supplied.

"Please what?"

"Please cut the noise," she said with the warmest of smiles, fake as it was.

"Whatever." Cain shook his head as if he found her both irritating and ridiculous. She searched for a witty retort but couldn't think of anything cutting enough to put him in his place.

Before she could respond, Cain returned to his own apartment and slammed the door.

"Well, well," Julia muttered under her breath as she closed her own door. Perhaps Cammie was right. This man desperately needed help, and she was just the woman to see to it.

She'd kill him with kindness if it was the last thing she ever did.

Inspired now, she took out her laptop and sat down on the sofa. Making herself comfortable, she stretched out her legs, crossing her ankles. Booting up her computer, she went to her blog and saw that only fifty people had logged in to read her latest post. So far her efforts weren't going to impress anyone. Most of those who read her blog were family and friends. The solitary comment had come from her mother.

Julia's fingers settled over the keyboard, and she typed away.

Julia's Blog

TWELVE DAYS OF CHRISTMAS

December 14

Meet Ebenezer

I'm wondering if anyone else has encountered a genuine curmudgeon this Christmas season? The reason I ask is because I believe Ebenezer Scrooge lives in my apartment building. To be fair, he hasn't shared his views on Christmas with me personally. One look and I can tell this guy doesn't possess a single ounce of holiday spirit. He just so happens to live directly across the hallway from me, so I've run into him on more than one occasion. To put it mildly, he's not a happy man.

Just this morning I discovered he was something else:

A thief.

I caught him pilfering my newspaper. Really, does it get much lower than that? Well, as a matter of fact, it does. This evening, not more than a few minutes ago, I was confronted by said neighbor demanding that I turn down the Christmas "racket." I happened to be singing. He claimed it sounded like someone was dying.

When I complained about him to a friend—and, okay, I'll admit I was pretty ticked off at the time—it came to me that this coldhearted "neighbor" is a living, breathing Scrooge.

My friend, who is near and dear to my heart, suggested **I kill him with kindness.**

So, my friends, I hope you'll join me in this little experiment. I fully intend to kill my surly neighbor with the love, joy, and fun of Christmas. Naturally, I will keep his identity confidential, referring to him only as Ebenezer.

I'm not exactly sure where to start. If you have thoughts or suggestions, please share them below. I'll be updating this blog every day until Christmas. Hopefully, by then, this Grinch's heart will have grown a few sizes.

My expectations are low.

I'm not convinced kindness can change a person.

We'll find out together.

I welcome your comments and ideas . . .

ABOUT THE AUTHOR

DEBBIE MACOMBER is a leading voice in women's fiction, with more than 200 million copies of her books in print worldwide. Twelve of her novels have hit #1 on the **New York Times** bestseller list, with three debuting at #1 on the **New York Times, USA Today,** and **Publishers Weekly** lists.

debbiemacomber.com
Facebook.com/debbiemacomberworld
Twitter: @debbiemacomber
Instagram: @debbiemacomber
Pinterest.com/macomberbooks